Welcome to the
Caribbean

True Tales from the Islands

ALAN BERRY

WestBow°
PRESS
A DIVISION OF THOMAS NELSON
& ZONDERVAN

WestBow Press books may be ordered through booksellers or by contacting:

WestBow Press
A Division of Thomas Nelson & Zondervan
1663 Liberty Drive
Bloomington, IN 47403
www.westbowpress.com
1 (866) 928-1240

ISBN: 978-1-4908-6461-7 (sc)
ISBN: 978-1-4908-6462-4 (hc)
ISBN: 978-1-4908-6460-0 (e)

Library of Congress Control Number: 2014922844

Print information available on the last page.

WestBow Press rev. date: 3/10/2015

Scripture taken from the King James Version of the Bible.

Contents

Preface

People have asked, "What is it like to be a missionary?" This book answers in part that question. As a missionary I have lived or visited the places mentioned. Except for the type of boat collision, I have experienced all events at least once, or many times. As far as the the boat collision; I have collided in a small dinghy against a larger boat, and went for a swim. I have seen pictures of a 27 foot boat underneath a fast moving catamaran. I have been within inches of a ship collision when I was in the Coast Guard.

This book is not about missionary endeavors per se, but events encountered on the mission field. These are things other than time spent studying/teaching/preaching the Word of God. I have never considered myself making a sacrifice being a missionary, but have considered it a challenge for the everyday living necessary to be on the mission field. For an American, most do not realize, that some of these things are "business as usual" and that is why I write.

One of the things I did on the mission field was to attempt the re-building of a 37' Jim Brown trimaran. There have been dinghies and models all along the way. My first boat was an

8' dinghy built in our basement while I was a senior in high school. My present boat is fiberglass built 20 years ago on the front porch. It has a 2.5hp engine. I can swim from it, fish or drift with the currents. I can go to a private beach if I desire. By not taking the cell phone, no one calls; no one comes to the door. It does what I built it to do. Lately I get to use it about two times a year.

Near the end of chapter two I mentioned stuff we had put into a professional storage place. Coming back from our first term we didn't collect our stored stuff right away, and there was a fire at the storage place. The only thing returned to us, were our wedding pictures, burnt around the edges. We did collect insurance.

Thirty years later we were contacted by a man who thirty years ago had bought the Coast Guard sword at a flea market. It had U.S Coast Guard on it, and my name. Over the years he had asked different Coast Guard people how to contact me. Finally, on the internet, he found our web site and has now returned the sword (minus the handle, obviously burnt). At the end of the book I mention the fire.

Names and dates have been changed to confuse readers who know me, and perhaps were present when these things occurred. In case you are in the know, and say that didn't happen here in St. Vincent, then it happened in Majuro (or vice versa), or possibly somewhere else. People who have read parts of this have asked, "Is this true?" Except for the fictional characters, and fictional story line, the events are true.

The acts are real. There are things left out, that we did.

Our dog carried the name given in the story. He lived to be fourteen human years. Our other dog, in the Marshall Islands, was eaten by the neighbors, evidently.

To think that my life has had some exceptional moments would even go back in my very early years. I am not sure what grade in school I was; third or fourth grade comes to mind. I was in the front seat, without a seat belt in those days, and sitting with my older brother. It was extremely foggy and we couldn't see more than a car length in front. I think we were on a 50mph, two lane road, but my dad was going much slower because the visibility was so bad. We were in a straight stretch approaching where we would turn up the country road to our house. After experiencing it, I remember my dad telling the story to someone later on.

My dad said, "For some reason I felt the need to pull over, off the road." So he did. We sat there just a very short time. We were off the paved road, on the grassy shoulder. Out of the fog came two cars, one passing the other, taking up the entire road coming almost straight at us. They were there, and gone in a split second. They had to be doing 50mph in the opposite direction. There would have been no avoiding them if we were still out on the road. We pulled back on the road, and continued home. God has protected my life on numerous occasions as you shall read.

To every endeavor of mankind there are obstacles, some great, and some small. Man is not remembered for failing to overcome those obstacles, but for persevering and overcoming them. Many times it seems as if there were a malevolent design behind these obstacles. I believe there is. In Mexico this would be called Diablo; on planes we called them gremlins. The Bible calls the mastermind, Satan, and his followers, demons. Be aware that the opposition is bent upon destruction; not just temporary derailment, or discouragement. The full sinister force is not felt at times because of the grace of God.

This book is not intended to be theological, but as you read you will find that this fatal opposition takes on many forms, sometimes human, sometimes things, sometimes animals, and sometimes inanimate objects. Satan desires nothing except to destroy mankind.

Enjoy.

Dedication Page

I dedicate this to the God who created the earth and the sky and is in complete control here on this earth. He wrote a book to communicate His love towards us, the Bible. He sent His son, Jesus, to pay for my sins and yours. Except for the changes God has made in my life, this book would be entirely different. Maybe it would not be written at all.

I dedicate this to my wife, Beverly, who has been with me for most of these events. Over 44 years of marriage, most of our time has been outside the United States. It has not been easy. We lived in a converted bus for a year and a half, raising support to go to the mission field. Six months after we arrived in Majuro high waves took out every house in our neighborhood, and ours alone stood. Later we moved into a house with only walls around the bathroom. Bookcases and curtains formed the other walls. For some time we had electricity only between midnight and 6am. Pipe water was on for only one hour a day.

The longest we have lived anywhere in our lives has been in Barrouallie, St. Vincent and the Grenadines. We have (so far) lived in two different houses there in Barrouallie. In St. Vincent we have moved five (5) times. My wife is still with me.

I dedicate this to all our supporting churches and pastors. Some pastors have been supporting pastors from the time they took us on initially for support, until now. That support spans over 38 years. It is their prayers and support that has allowed us to serve on the mission field. Some have made trips to our mission field. So they probably have a clearer picture of what the mission field is really like. Some pastors and personal supporters have a present front row seat in heaven.

I dedicate this to those we have ministered to over the years, especially those who accepted Christ as Savior and followed in believer's baptism. They have helped us move from one location to another, been there when we have needed comfort, and encouraged us in the ministry.

One day when "time turns into eternity", those in the Marshall Islands, and St. Vincent & the Grenadines, and America, will gather around the throne of God to share our experience together to His honor and glory.

Chapter One

Welcome - The Plane Ride Down - Layover in Barbados – Arrival

Stan and Marcy Kerry had dreamed of exploring the world on a boat. They had come to the Caribbean and worked hard on making the boat seaworthy. Now they were out sailing and the weather had gone bad. For some reason the phrase kept going through his mind, "Welcome to the Caribbean." They had heard and repeated that phrase every time something went wrong. From the beginning, it seemed as if things went wrong, and that phrase would be repeated. But they had finally launched this boat and were able to cruise the Caribbean Sea.

They found themselves on a sea anchor, in the open sea, with winds in the upper thirties and gusting. Waves had increased to 5-8 feet with occasional 10 footers. Most waves were white capped and breaking. What a welcome to a place they had so much wanted to visit!

The sea anchor is like a small parachute deployed underwater. It attaches to the boat by a single line. A swivel allows it to twist and turn without kinking the rope. If properly deployed, it will hold a boat steady in a position facing the wind and waves. It is not attached to the bottom. Wind driven current, tidal current, sea currents, will all play into which way the boat will drift. The sea anchor just lets the boat face the waves and wind.

Stan had gone up on deck to check the boat. Seas were not that big at eight feet, but their fetch gave no chance for rest, and made for a complete lack of comfort. Marcy was still slightly seasick but okay. She was not in the mood to cook, or to eat. She was lying on the port bunk. She had rigged a canvas preventer: a square piece of canvas screwed under the length of the mattress, and tied to the side of the boat. It formed something like a hammock, which prevented her from being dumped on the floor, if there was a sudden lurch of the boat. She had tied a bucket near her head, within easy reach-"just in case."

With the wind from the south, Stan began to realize they might be in for some rough weather for a while. An "almost hurricane" had practically formed on top of them without too much warning. It was mostly blown past. They had just decided to slow down the boat and take it easy. They were bobbing up and down with the sea anchor holding them in position, no sails, tiller tied down, out of the normal transit lane. They were drifting because of the wind current backward NNW. It was not the direction they wanted to take, but dictated to by the size of the waves and strength of the sea. They wanted to work their way back towards the islands, instead of being blown farther into the Caribbean Sea. Wind and sea were their main concerns, and a twenty six foot boat was not powerful enough to make much headway. He could not set sail until the wind *dropped; then it promised to be a wet beat to windward. They were not close to any nearby island.*

Marcy was almost seasick, and that left Stan the only one to manage the boat. They had plenty of sea room, and were just holding their own. In the next twenty-four hours this storm would be history, they hoped, and they could shake out the reef and begin to get to the next island.

Stan went to the mast so he could see the shine of the running lights, and was sighting up the mast to check it out for any signs of flexing. The small engine in Susan (the boat they were on) would be of little value in these conditions, and they would need the sails to set a course that would take them back to land.

He was just studying the wake and trying to judge just how fast they were drifting, when he heard a noise to windward. He turned and saw an aluminum beam coming over the waves right for him. His reflex was to jump! When he came down he hit neither the deck of his own boat, nor the water, but landed in a net and tumbled over and over.

Even with the screeching of the wind, he could hear some major crashing and thumping going on. He could hear Marcy screaming but couldn't figure out where she was. Stan wasn't sure where he was. When he stopped rolling he realized he was lying on this large net and there were some unfamiliar voices screaming around him. He had landed on the front deck of a very large catamaran, which evidently had passed right over the top of his boat and had hardly slowed down.

While rebuilding Susan, they encountered difficulties, and strange happenings. As Stan assessed the situation, he thought,

"Welcome to the Caribbean." Now he had to figure out what his next step would be. The mast from Susan was draped across the front of the catamaran, and pretzeled out of shape. There was an obvious bend in the front beam of the cat, the forestay was slacked and he had no idea what boat this was. Then Stan saw I-See, the Rastafarian. The unforgettable scar on his face was instantly recognizable.

On the plane flight down to Barbados, Stan had noticed two other Americans that seemingly were traveling together, yet around security and the check-in lines, they made sure they were not together. He saw them talking together at the snack shop. They were dressed in shorts and t-shirts, with gold necklaces and rings on every finger. They fit the profile of what he thought of as a "druggie". Their age was in the mid-twenties and not very communicative.

Stan was hoping to find some information, and when he ended up sitting next to the one called Ben, he struck up a conversation.

"First time to the Caribbean?" asked Stan

"No." replied Ben

"Where you headed"

"Barbados for now."

"Business or pleasure?"

"Both." Ben grinned.

"What kind of job allows you to combine the two? Seems like a job I should pursue."

"Import, export."

"What products?"

"Whatever the going commodity is."

"Must be nice."

"Oh, it is really nice. I like the hours and, the adventure, and the profit is generally good."

"Where are you staying?"

"A friend's place."

But Stan could never get Ben to tell him what was in the Caribbean that would need exporting to the States. In fact, Ben didn't seem to really want to talk, so Stan picked the most comfortable position he could and tried to get some rest.

At Barbados, you have to exit the plane and the airport terminal. Then you go back to the terminal to re-check your baggage for your connecting flight. Stan picked up his bags, and was in line checking through customs. He noticed a lady in another line, who was being asked about some items, when she suddenly bolted for the door and left her suitcase! The stunned customs officer just folded up the suitcase, and set it on the ground and waited on the next flier.

Stan collected his suitcase from the customs people and walked through the same door the lady had run through, which was the only door they could use. He found himself on the street, with a row of taxis.

Even though he was on a connecting flight to St. Vincent, and his passport was so stamped, he could have taken a taxi and gone someplace, anyplace in Barbados. Stan couldn't believe this was happening. There were no arrows on the concrete, but plenty of people kept announcing and directing foot traffic. He was tempted to just get in a taxi and see what would happen. The area he had stepped into had a vast roof stretching over the taxi area and down both sides of the building.

While walking outside he noticed that Ben and David were standing and talking to a Rasta man with long dreadlocks. He wore shorts, a T-shirt, and what Stan would consider shower shoes. There was no missing the gold necklaces hanging down his front. It reminded Stan of the Olympic gold medals, but he was sure that this was not a real gold necklace he was looking at. The Rasta man looked skinny and underfed. If Stan had moved a little closer, he would have noticed the permanently red eyes that seem to come with habitual use of marijuana. Evidently, someone had slashed him down the side of his head; his dreadlocks covered most of the scar, but not all.

Rastafarianism is a Caribbean cult based loosely on the worship of Haile Selassie, Emperor of Ethiopia (1930-1974). Rastafarians think of him as, somehow, Jesus Christ re-incarnated on the earth. Each island promotes their variations, and beliefs. In one island, they are known for selling the best produce - they steal from the best gardens. Another island, they are known for their hard work and well kept gardens. Another island they are unkempt and dirty. Bob Marley from Jamaica made the Rastas a little better known in America and England. But, still, many have never heard of Rastafaria. The one thing they all seem to have in common, they smoke marijuana, and most are vegetarians. The men have the long dreadlocks, and clothing with red, yellow and green predominate. They even have modified words so they have their own lingo.

Rastafarianism started in Jamaica, and as it spread over the Caribbean, to became the backbone for the Caribbean drug trade. At first it was just marijuana, but with Colombia just south of them, the islands provided a pipeline for the harder drugs north.

The European countries, who owned the islands in years gone by, continued to send tourists. The Caribbean became a major distribution point for the drug trade.

Tourists attempting to take drugs home had/have mixed results. The very people who sold them the drugs could/would turn them into the police. Arrests were made on people already on the plane. The tourist was taken off the plane, along with his bags. He now faced jail, or a hefty fine. If he was fortunate, he could leave the same day on a later flight.

The police were making arrests, and doing their part on the "war on drugs." The druggies stayed in business and paid the police to leave them alone. For a policeman, that payment sometimes was more than his salary. The tourist, now in jail, didn't get a refund.

Many arrests made had to have an informer.

With the right contacts, one could make a fortune. However, you were dealing in death. Either the end user, or the very people who grew the plant, or the middle man were in fierce competition. When a competitor steals from your field, you cannot go to the police and complain. Fields were generally guarded, with illegal guns. Some of those guns were homemade, but could be deadly. More than one "farmer" disappeared, or they found a body and didn't know who it was.

There were fishermen who delivered the drugs to northern island countries. Or they were meeting up with boats in international waters. What better way to up the profits but by eliminating the "middle man", and stealing his boat in the process? Many a Vincentian went to sea, to fish, they claimed. They ended up missing because the drug deal went bad. They and their boat just didn't return. People dealing in drugs, were dealing in death.

Ben and Dave were going to head farther south in a private speed boat, conveniently stolen, and mostly equipped with stolen items. Their identities would be changed. I-See, the Rastafarian who met them at the curb of the airport, had a taxi waiting to take them to another location. He had arranged all other details as well. They would arrive on a moonless night in Venezuela, on a deserted beach and disappear with some of their local connections. They would use a stolen yacht capable of making a fast trip north. In the past they had used power boats, but the Coast Guard and police were scrutinizing those boats now. For the first time they were looking at stealing a large catamaran the owner had just left at a marina. Normally it would sit out the hurricane season in Venezuela while the owner went back north, and then be used when the owner returned during the tourist season. False documents for the boat had already been arranged, and they knew the owner had booked his flight to leave in the evening. By the time his plane cleared the runway they would have the boat already out of its slip and headed for the place where the drugs would be loaded. His friendly boat captain had been well paid for all the information they needed. The boat would not be reported missing for a long time.

The setup was very simple. No one knew who was the master planner, or who were all involved. One group stole the boat and delivered it to the next group at a particular place. The growers would load pickup trucks and have no idea where they were headed. The pickup truck would head to a deserted beach and await a boat. They just had to follow directions, and they would be well paid.

Their cover was simple; they were the tourists who had a yacht with a captain and crew. The boat would be abandoned or sold depending on how things worked out at the delivery end. Hopefully by the time it could be traced, they would be long gone. If caught, they wouldn't lose anything, as the boat didn't belong to them. If it was seized and sold at auction, too bad for the owner who had no idea his boat was going to be involved in such purposes.

Meanwhile, Stan noticed the airline desks and signs down to his right. He assumed that is where he had to head. Stan hadn't actually exited the airport. He was still under the canopy, but felt like he re-entered the airport. He went to the LIAT check in counter to connect to the St. Vincent flight.

Layover in Barbados

Stan was going to find out that his confirmed LIAT ticket didn't mean anything. There was no space available on the plane and the other flights that night were filled as well. He was going to spend the night in Barbados, not at a nice hotel, down on the beach, but in the Bajan airport. LIAT did not so much as offer a drink. He had been bumped out of his confirmed ticket by the agent at the front desk. "Overbooked" she had said. Stan was adaptable to what was going to happen, but it didn't make him a happy customer. A night would be spent in the Barbados airport. LIAT would not provide him with accommodations, or food, or drink. He had arrived in Barbados on a different airline. "They" were not responsible.

Even with the arrival of a special flight, (just for the overbooked passengers) that still didn't get him on a flight out. It took out 48 passengers. There seemed to be that many still standing there with tickets in hand. He was just left standing at the airport, with no place to go. Stan went back out to the taxi area and he couldn't see a hotel in sight. None were close by, and he was not given any directions for hotel accommodations. He went back to the counter.

He was not the only one. He listened to the tales of woe as he stood next to the counter trying to figure out what he was going to do. He listened in on the following conversation:

"Your travel agent should have known that this flight was overbooked. He should have never given you a ticket for this flight." The Head ticket agent said to a customer.

"I am the travel agent and ten people, including the lady over there in the wheel chair are part of my travel group. I can guarantee you that we would have not bought tickets if this flight was flagged as full or overbooked." The customer replied heatedly. His group did not leave that night either.

Another conversation:

"Ma'am, we have spent over 8 hours on a plane, we have these two children, and you are telling me we can't get on the plane to St. Vincent?" A distraught father of two very tired children voiced his displeasure.

"Sorry sir, the plane is full." The ticket agent said curtly.

"Where can we go to spend the night?" The man further asked.

"Sorry sir, you came in on BWIA and therefore that is not our problem." The agent replied a little nicer this time.

"What about tomorrow?" The man asked.

The agent clearly said, "Our planes are booked full for tomorrow."

Stan took note, that none of them got on a plane out that night.

The agent, at Stan's insistence, had started a standby list. She really had no idea what to do with it. It became obvious that no one else was getting out that night. He asked what she was going to do. She stated she would start another list in the morning. Stan insisted that since his name was at the top of the list, that it remain there; first come, first served. There should be no new list, and those on the old list should get priority. Stan was telling her how to do her job, and she seemed to actually be listening!

On and on and on the stories continued, until Stan finally drifted off to find a comfortable place to spend the night.

He spent all night wandering around an empty terminal. Since he was not checked in, he couldn't go inside the terminal. In the waiting area there were some seats and benches. It was a humid, buggy wait for daybreak. The snack shops all closed up and only a few security people were around.

He did call Frazer and told him of the delay. "No problem, boss." was the reply.

When the airport closed at 10pm, they turned off the lights, and now Stan could not even see the mosquitoes that came for their blood transfusion. It is amazing how a little thing like a mosquito can turn paradise into a real miserable place, and it only took one. It becomes more annoying when they come one at a time.

The next morning, at 6:00am, he was the only person on standby, waiting at the desk. He was the only standby passenger, who got the one available seat, and flew into St. Vincent.

They re-weighed his bags. LIAT had a 40lb weight limit, which Stand had not anticipated. They also limited check through to one bag, Stan had two. Both bags were overweight. Stan paid over $300 for excess baggage. "Welcome to the Caribbean" he thought. He was given a seating ticket and now he could re-enter the security area, showing his passport and LIAT seating ticket. Then he went through another security check-in. This was not exactly a user friendly connection.

Fortunately he had time to call Frazer before he got on the plane. Even though he was sure he would be on the plane, it was delayed for several hours. By now he knew that LIAT didn't stand for "Leeward Island Air Transport," but Leave Island At Any Time! Hopefully he would not find the other meaning, "Luggage in Another Terminal."

This plane was the LIAT turbo prop and the seats were narrow, and the carryon luggage space was smaller than the other airlines he had traveled. His feet were on top of the carry-on suitcase. It wouldn't fit in the overhead bin. They almost took it from him and made him check it in as baggage. But he would not part with it – it had needed tools, spare cash, spare clothes, snack foods.

The plane wasn't plugged into a generator. The inside of plane became like a sauna until the plane was airborne. There was just no way to really get comfortable as he tried to sleep. The seats would not recline. The flight was without any meals. So Stan would not get breakfast and he couldn't even get a free drink! Not even a glass of water. Forty-Eight people crammed into a commuter prop plane, without service.

Most airlines offered a drink, and it would cost you out of your pocket. Snacks were not included in the ticket. You would have to pay for them also. LIAT was not offering snacks or drinks at any price.

Stan was now in St. Vincent. After 38 hours of flying and layovers he was definitely tired, but he had arrived. Mostly layovers and delayed flights had made the trip already seem more like a nightmare than a dream, but he was committed to what lay ahead. He had left 5" of snow and was now the envy of everybody in the office.

Stan was in his early thirties, and had for years wondered about how to "follow the good life" as he envisioned it. What was to unfold before him was going to be part good, and some parts downright scary, though he didn't know that at the time. But it was a part of life, and one that he and Marcy had willfully chosen.

At 5'4" he found himself in company with tall thin people getting off the plane and heading for the terminal. He thought, "This must be Basketball country," and yet at the time, there were only two courts on the whole island. Eventually one NBA player and three WNBA players would come from St. Vincent and the Grenadines.

Stan had connected his flight through New York. Most of the passengers were Vincies returning to St. Vincent or those going back to visit their homeland. Later he would find out one half of the citizens of the country lived outside St. Vincent and the Grenadines (SVG).

When they opened the door of the plane, and Stan disembarked from the air conditioned plane it was like walking into a blast furnace. The heat was rising off the tarmac and engulfing him. For nine o'clock in the morning it already seemed plenty hot. The fifty yards to the building looked like 500 yards. He hoped that he would acclimate quickly. The sun was shining so bright it actually was hurting his head. He sought the confines of the building for shade.

The terminal looked like someone had made major mistake in its coloring. It was neither yellow, nor orange, but something in between, leaning towards the orange. He had never seen an airline terminal painted this color in all his travels. The inside had the same color and made him uncomfortable.

However, much to his dismay, the building was worse than outside. There was no air conditioning and no fans and no breeze. It had not been designed for air conditioning. Fans had never been put in place. What use to be breeze ways and windows were now blocked with non opening, non - see through windows, because of the new security measures.

Walls were erected to obscure and keep out potential problems. Stan would never know if the walls kept out potential problems, but the arrangement now kept out any flow of air. The almost orange walls seemed to close in around him. It was about 85/85 (85 degrees and 85% humidity). Standing in line to check through immigration without air conditioning, was like being in an oven. The sweat was dripping off his face and it was running down his back. He was beginning to wonder if he was cooked through, or just "over easy."

Frazer told him he would be at the airport and everything would be ok. However, as he was separated from the rest of the world by walls and doors, and he had to get through customs and immigration first. He stepped up to the counter and this well dressed gentleman in black pants and shoes, with a white, long sleeve shirt and black tie was all business. There was no friendly "good to see you", or "welcome to St. Vincent". He noticed that despite being indoors, the man was wearing sunglasses. He would remember that later, when he heard the Prime Minister during a news broadcast, mention that anyone who wore sunglasses inside had an attitude problem.

The man politely took his passport and then asked him a question. He knew that this was an English speaking country. He knew that what the man spoke should be English. But, what this man spoke to him could just as well have been Greek, or any other language. After the man repeated the question three times Stan still had no idea what English dialect he was speaking. He wanted to laugh. He knew he should understand the man, but it made no sense to him at all. He then remembered his letter from the owner of the boat and quickly gave it to the immigration agent. Al had thoughtfully prepared a letter detailing they were to stay with Frazer until they could get the boat in the water, and then they would return the boat to Miami. The immigration officer read the letter and finally stamped his passport and waved him through.

Now he was going to find out the other meaning of LIAT. Their tickets said Leeward Islands Airlines Transport, but logic said simply: "Luggage In Another Territory." Not just his clothes, but all their tools and spare parts he had brought down were in another terminal. Hopefully they would all show up in a couple of days. All he had was his carryon luggage. He reminded himself that he had paid an extra $300 for them to lose his luggage.

Arrival

With everything that had happened to him, Stan began to doubt if Frazer would be there to meet him on the other side of the doors. But having nowhere else to go, he stepped back into the sunlight of St. Vincent and was immediately bombarded with "Need a taxi, Mon?"

"No, I'm here looking for Frazer" And he had no more said those words and realized he didn't have a clue what Frazer looked like; no picture, no verbal description. He was told

"No problem, Mon. He'll be here. If not, check the marina at Calliaqua; just ask a taxi to take you there."

But Frazer wasn't to be found. With no idea where Frazier lived other than "Prospect" and he didn't have a clue where that was. He also had no street address. He later found there were no street addresses. Stan had no idea where to go. He didn't even see a phone around the departure area. He turned down many taxi offers, and by the time most of the passengers had cleared the terminal, a white Corolla came under the awning in the taxi area and a man stepped out. He was dressed in some slick looking clothes. Stan couldn't get over the fact that he had on a long sleeved shirt and was wearing a tie. He was as dark as the blackness of the night sky, with pearly white teeth and eyes that studied everything around them. At about 6'3" and skinny as a rail he wondered if he was looking at a man who ran the marina or a professional basketball player. It was Frazer.

That first stop was Kentucky Fried Chicken (the only American Franchise on the island) for a hearty meal that Stan so deserved after going hungry for hours.

Marcy's Ticket

The second stop was a local travel agent in town where he checked on his wife's ticket for the coming week. He had come ahead to scout out the place and call back and order anything they may need.

Marcy's ticket was for the next week, with identical flight times, identical connections. When he asked the head ticket agent in Barbados, she was NOT listed, not even on standby. She had typed in some figures into the computer but he could not see the screen. But, having bought the tickets, he was visibly upset that her name wasn't even in the computer

So from the travel agents' office in St. Vincent he called Barbados and asked for the head ticket agent by name.

"Betsy, I'm Stan Kerry, remember me from last night?"

"Yes."

"Could you check again to see if my wife is on the flight next week?"

Pause - "No sir, she is not."

"Would you care to explain that to me and the ticket agent here, why you don't have her name in the computer? We are looking at the computer screen and it has her name listed with a confirmed ticket?"

Long Pause. "You sure, sir?"

"Yes, and I expect you to do something about it".

Before it was over he had also called LIAT in Antigua and sent them a fax and emails. In the end when Marcy came a week later, she was almost escorted through the airport in Barbados.

While waiting for Marcy, Stan would work on the boat.

Arnos Vale airport

Chapter Two

How it All Started – St. Vincent and the Grenadines

Al met Stan and Marcy at the yacht club after a race one day. Stan and Marcy were sailing on a friend's boat for the race. Al had a racing machine that was doing well, with a polished crew. They were at the yacht club and discussing the maneuver used to beat Al's boat at the finish. The boat Stan and Marcy were on tacked over to starboard just before the finish line, making Al's boat have to give way and go behind. Then Stan and Marcy pulled up almost straight into the wind and had enough momentum to finish just a half boat length ahead.

Al was not happy but impressed, with their maneuver. Out of the whole fleet the two boats were rated the same, and it would be simple, the first over the line would take the upper place in the standings. In this case, it was not for first place, but just a sweet victory, to beat a boat rated identical, and by such a close margin, just because they knew what their boat would do in that situation.

Al was a good sport, and readily likeable. He wanted to talk to these people who had beaten his well trained crew. He even tried to recruit Stan and Marcy off their friend's boat.

When Stan and Marcy first met Al after that race, they thought he was a little overweight. But when they sat down at the table to talk they were aware that what they thought was a little extra weight, was rock solid muscle. His shirt sleeve was almost too small to get on, and hugged his biceps. Al spent some serious time at the gym lifting weights. When he folded his arms across his chest he looked like the "Mr. Clean" they had seen on bottles in the grocery store. One would not want to meet Al in a dark alley some day that was for sure.

They found out that he was into writing computer programs for monster machines that took up entire rooms. But, he had a mind that would allow him to write 200 lines of source code without putting it on paper, and once printed out, could easily spot any errors. With a very good salary, he had invested in different things. Some of them were in the stock market, but he bought and sold houses, cars, and any other thing he could find that seemed like a good deal. Drug auctions were his specialty, and he could calculate on his feet when to go for a bid, or bail out as the item was not worth where the bidding was going. He had bought a farm where he stored stuff until he re-sold it. Some of it was even under an army tent – also bought at an auction.

"What was the longest race you two have been involved in?" Al asked.

"We raced Annapolis Newport Race last year." Stan replied.

"That race had a lot of withdrawals." Al said, deep in thought.

"We weren't one of them."

"Had any problems?"

"Hatch got ripped off, and we had to jury rig it."

"How did you do that?"

"Well the owner had only one screwdriver and no hammers, and we had to improvise. We found a section of the forward bunk that was slightly bigger than the hatch area, and we were fortunate it fit without the need of a saw. We took two screws out of the six holding down each shelf in the galley, and sealed the hatch as best we could. Had to be careful not to step on the hatch as we felt it would probably break. We even tied some spare life jackets in the front part of the hatch to deflect any wave that might hit"

"Any experience on major repairs, or fixing more serious things?" Al asked, seemingly impressed.

"Stan worked part time in the local yard fixing boats. I worked with him some on the weekends. We build furniture for a hobby." Marcy said, bragging about her husband.

"Own a boat?"

"No, we don't own one, but we hope to some day. We hope to go cruising, see the Caribbean, maybe go through to the Pacific and see all the islands and blue sea that we can."

They began to talk about boats and dreams of sailing in the tropics. Al had taken his second boat down to the Caribbean and had stored it from time to time on land, and returned in successive years to pick it up and sail it. Now it was in St.

Vincent, and Al was unable to bring the boat back. It had set for almost three years, and Al's working hours would not allow him the time off he needed. He realized there had to be a better way to get back to it. Getting it to Miami would be a big start.

"I actually have two boats you know." Al said off handedly, looking for their reaction to his statement.

"How do you afford it?" Stan asked. He was shocked with that comment. Boats were generally expensive and how could Al afford one, let alone two:

"The boat I race is here, where I can use it after hours, and week -ends. But, I have a small cruiser down in the Caribbean. I went to a drug auction and bought this 26 feet cruiser; all fiberglass, with sails, radio, and even had the galley dishes and pans. I considered it a good deal for less than $4,000. It was in Key West, so I took off a month and went south. The weather closed in north of me and it would be difficult to fight the wind to get back to the states. I kept going south and left it in the Windward Islands. My next vacation I picked it up where I left off and took it all the way to Trinidad."

"Seems like a great opportunity." Marcy said thoughtfully.

"Well the problem has come up, that I still haven't got it back to the U.S. I've even tried to sell it down there, but no takers. I would like it back up here in the states, maybe back here in NY."

"So why don't you go down and get it?" Stan questioned.

"The vacation time just hasn't been available. I can't afford to take a vacation. While I am making the money I need, I just can't get off." Al said.

"So you need someone to go and pick it up?"

"Well, it will need more than just someone who can sail. It probably needs repairs, but I kept putting it off. By now I am sure it will have to be fixed, before being put back in the water. Maybe you would be interested?"

"That seems like a great idea. Stan can fix anything, and I am sure we could sail it up." Marcy spoke up already excited.

"But we only get two weeks of vacation a year. Not to mention we don't really have the kind of income that would allow us to live in the Caribbean. Not sure how this could possibly work out." Stan said, with disappointment in his voice.

"Are you adventuresome?" Al asked.

"In what way?" Marcy said.

"Well, there is a cheap way to stay where the boat is." Al replied.

"What is that?" Marcy said.

"You could stay with a Vincy family."

"Oh." Stan said.

"Yea, the guy who runs the marina said he had an extra bedroom, and if I came back and needed a place for awhile I could stay with him. I stayed with him after the boat was pulled out of the water. I stayed for a couple of weeks before I flew out." Al stated.

"That sounds like a workable idea." Marcy said, getting more excited again.

"It sounds like it would be … ah… really different." Stan said more hesitantly.

"Guaranteed it will be different. I stayed with them for several days getting the boat out of the water and stored so things would not get lost or stolen while I was gone. I built a storage box, which could be locked securely off the boat. When I was ready to go, LIAT went on strike and I was stuck for a few more days before leaving. Frazer's wife is an excellent cook. She has been to the states and understands us Americans." Al said cheerfully.

It all sounded good to Stan but he needed time to think about it. He didn't want to set about on a fool's errand "We will talk about it, but don't lay awake at night expecting us to take you up on this."

"Well, I keep looking for someone who could do this. Please take my card and give me a call if you decide you could do it. Remember, it may entail some work on the boat, before you ever set sail." Al said, extracting a business card from his shirt pocket.

With that simple conversation, the business card was posted on the fridge by Marcy, and they got to walk past it every day. However, the Caribbean seemed so far away. They never made that call, days turned into weeks and weeks into months.

Little did they know what the future was going to bring.

For Stan and Marcy this was the dream of a lifetime. They had messed about on boats before they met, and even after they were married, they had pursued what boating interests they could afford. A car, and a mortgage, had not diminished their dream, and they did not want to give up on it. But the business card on the fridge did not seem to hold any promises to fulfill their dream.

After the summer racing season was over they had returned to the cold offices of New York and the daily commute.

Stan's mother died and after the estate was settled, as some would say, Stan had a good nest egg. Being the only child, he had inherited a large sum of cash, and the sale of her house added to that. They decided to sell their house and move to an apartment closer to the city. It just might save them enough money to start looking at a boat. Much to their shock they sold the house in the first week, with a 30 day notice to vacate for the buyers to move in.

The next day they received their notices that their services at the company were no longer needed. It was downsizing, and both of them were no longer needed. They were given severance pay, and that was that. Being homeless and jobless seemed a major event in their lives.

Then they remembered the business card of Al's and decided this was the opportunity they were seeking. Especially if Al would allow them to continue to live on the boat on their return to the states until they could find housing or jobs. Al readily agreed and they were soon packing and storing stuff for their exodus to sunny paradise.

Packing began with five piles.

They decided to have a yard sale. Stan's collection of Louis Lamour books should get them some money, and at $5.00 apiece they would make over $500. Marcy gave up her Anne Livingston collection and so from those piles the yard sale got going. Of course all the yard equipment, rakes, shovels, mowers, etc. added to that pile. It was an amazing yard sale. Nobody was interested in the Louis Lamoure books.

The second pile went to the Salvation Army. And that pile got larger after the yard sale. What didn't sell, they were not going to keep and saw no sense in throwing it away.

They decided to put some things in professional storage, wedding dress, pictures, Stan's racing bike, the boat he built in High School and other things that were worth more as mementos than their monetary value. Stan's trophies collected over the years and his Coast Guard Sword when he graduated from the Coast Guard Academy.

Al gave them some ideas and Al shipped a couple of small heavy boxes of tools by a freight forwarder out of New York for them.

The fifth pile was trash. It took several trips to the dump to finally clear out the house. When they left for the last time there was a note of sadness as the rooms were clean and they flipped off the light switch for the last time and went towards their new life. It was one of those emotional events that cannot be explained, it can only be felt by those who have gone through it.

Stan was going to fly down first and get a feel of "The lay of the land." Marcy was going to come a week later. She was going to stay at her sister's after Stan left. The vehicle was going to be stored at her sister's house, hopefully in useable condition when they returned, whenever that would be.

Saint Vincent and the Grenadines

Located in the southern Caribbean, Saint Vincent is a small island 11x20 miles. The only Windward Island farther south is Grenada, made famous by Cuba building an airstrip and the Communist party trying to take over the government. The United States sent troops and intervened before either were completed.

The Windward Islands form a barrier between the Caribbean Sea and the Atlantic Ocean. Individual islands are not that far apart. On a clear day one could sail from island to island down or up the chain by just looking.

St. Vincent, as do the other islands, has a volcano starting at sea level, towering 4,000 feet in the air. St. Vincent is only 80 miles away from Granada, with Bequia, Mustique, Canouan, Union Island, Mayreau and Carriacou in between. On a clear day you can see all these islands at once. It is hard to get lost. A navigator could get by with just a good pair of eyes.

Occasionally Sahara desert dust blows in and obscures visibility. It settles in like a fog. There have been some fishermen who have run out of gas looking to get back in to St. Vincent. The most astonishing thing occurred when locust from Africa came on the jet stream and deposited themselves all over the Caribbean islands. The one thing that kept them from having complete crop devastation was the critters did not re-produce. They just died. The sea gulls had something extra on their menu for a few days.

A person wanting to island hop and check out the Caribbean; St. Vincent is a good place to start. Much of the trip can be sailed on the leeward side of the islands. The Atlantic waves have lost their energy on the windward side of the island, so one is sailing in almost protected waters on the leeward side. The wave height is greatly reduced. Sailing close in to the islands, one doesn't have the wind, as it is blocked by the intervening island. Sailing farther out one gets bigger waves and more wind. A compromise is sought by all who sail; where there is enough wind to make good progress, and not enough waves to be uncomfortable.

Saint Vincent politically stretches south to Grenada. It includes some famous sailing areas. Bequia has an annual Easter sailing regatta. Tobago Keys is considered one of the best dive spots in the Caribbean. Canouan has a towering volcano dome, and a five star hotel. Union Islands boasts a one runway airport, and a quaint friendly atmosphere.

A volcanic island, St. Vincent had its last eruption in 1979. Most of the beaches in St. Vincent are black sand beaches. While most beaches in the Grenadines are white. There are many scenic coves for anchorage all up and down the area, some are accessible only by boat. While all beaches are public property, there are several areas where the land leading to the beach is privately owned. They can't stop people from being on the beach, but they can stop people from walking on their property.

Some bays are totally secluded, with a small stretch of sand between the ocean and the towering cliffs behind them.

This is the island where Marcy and Stan were coming to work on the boat *Susan* and do some sightseeing.

Frazer's Home

Frazer took him to his home, and showed him their room. Typical of West Indian homes, the guest room was small and had no closet. He would live out of his suitcase. However, there was no place but on the bed to lay the suitcase. There was a small table he could put some small stuff on, and slide the suitcase under the bed. There was an overhead light with about a 40 watt light bulb. He couldn't lie in bed and read very comfortably. There were no lamps in the room and the walls were dark blue.

The bed was a foam mattress with slats underneath. A well worn 4" foam doesn't give much of a beauty rest, but he solaced himself that this was training for moving aboard the boat. After lying in the bed for awhile, if he couldn't get to sleep immediately, he could count the slats underneath, as he waited for sleep to come.

The bathroom had the sink out in the hallway. There was no mirror over the sink, or lights in the area. The commode and shower each had their separate door. He found taking a shower without getting his clothes or towel wet was a real art. But taking his clothes and towel with him into the shower was better than stepping out naked into the hallway. The lack of ventilation in the shower area guaranteed that you were sweating by the time you could get dressed enough to get the door open and step out. Which almost made him wonder about why take a shower in the first place. All light switches for the bathroom area were out in the hallway. There were no receptacles in the bathroom area at all. Which is just as well, his electric shaver was 110v and the household current was 220v. He would need a transformer to get it to work.

There was no hot water in the shower, or at the sink. The left side of the faucet was just decoration. It didn't turn the water on or off. It had never been connected. There was no hot water. In the early morning the water was really cold. All pipes to the house lay on the ground. By late afternoon they soaked up the sun's rays, and the water would be lukewarm or sometimes hot water.

Even though it was still morning, he opted to go to bed. Frazer showed him how to pull the mosquito netting over the bed and mentioned that it was a good thing that malaria was unknown in St. Vincent. There was no fan in the room and the heat frustrated him. But somehow he managed to take a short nap, as miserable as it was. He set an alarm and woke up before lunch time. He even tried the shower to get the "stickies" off his body and to feel better than the inside of a gym sock.

The First Meal

Estella, Frazier's wife, had fixed a really nice dish of paleau, a dish of chicken and rice, flavored nicely with hot sauce. He was to learn later, she liked that hot sauce more than most Vincies and generously poured it on the plate.

Estella was not as tall as her husband, but was as thin as he was. She was quite talkative, and a very good organizer as Stan would notice. The children were kept on a routine that monitored their TV time, their play time, and their study time. She didn't allow any back talk, and disrespectful attitudes. Every night she checked their homework, which took priority over TV, sports, friends and almost anything else. Every morning their uniforms and shoes were ready for the closest military inspection that he had ever seen. There was much communication between children and adults in the household.

The children, Kesron 7, Estelita 9, and Julitha 13, had come home for lunch in their nice school uniforms and sat politely down. They had a different school system than in the states, but he really liked the idea of school uniforms. He found out later that if you "knew", you could tell which school each student came from. He was impressed. They all seemed to talk at once, and he had trouble keeping track of the many conversations going on. As an only child who grew up in a home where "silence was golden." He found this to be a stark contrast to his background, and interesting. There was also the fact that they were talking in "dialect", which he couldn't follow at all. It reminded him of the customs man at the airport. At times the conversation would stop and he would realize they were talking to him, and he had no clue as what question they had asked. It could have been anything from "Please pass the mustard," to "Do you have any children?" He only knew they were speaking to him, because all conversation had stopped, and all eyes were on him. He sat there feeling really stupid.

As they were talking, Stan realized that he was watching Estella pour the last of the lemonade into a glass, and realized he was only going to get just one, cold, drink.

The air was so humid you could almost stir it with a spoon. There were no fans and no air conditioning here. The sweat did not evaporate; it collected in puddles on your body, and then ran the direction gravity pulls everything, down. He had a river flowing down his back, and realized he was dripping under his armpits, and he was hoping the drops on his nose would not fall into the paleau. Paleau was a Caribbean dish, with basically flavored rice and chicken. It was generally flavored with curry sauce, and some liked it with more sauce than others. He was not worried about whether he would like the food or not, he was afraid he would just pass out from the heat. Even though they had stopped at KFC earlier, he was still hungry.

Every plate was filled in the kitchen. Therefore dinner was in front of you; one plate, one time. He found out later this was a polite way of saying there were no seconds on the food. They said grace, another difference between how he grew up, and this West Indian's home. They began to eat.

While that glass of lemonade looked inviting, one taste of the paleau and he realized he had better wait until the end of the meal to drink. Once he started drinking, there would be no end. He remembered Estella pouring out the last of the lemonade. The paleau was highly seasoned. He would find out later, that of all the paleau he ever ate, the Frazer's spiced it the hottest of all.

Of course what he did not know was that the glass did not contain lemonade, but Ginger Beer. It is really not a beer, but it is made of ginger, and again, Estella really liked to spice up her ginger beer, more than any other West Indian he would ever meet.

While he was digging through the plate of paleau he realized that not only was he hot on the outside, he was now beginning to burn on the inside. From the time it was in his mouth, to the bottom of his stomach he could feel this river of fire. However, he was their guest, and not having a clue of where else to stay, he had made his mind up to enjoy this Vincy culture and adapt as best he could.

After some pleasant talk, and careful wiping of the sweat off his face, he finally reached the bottom of the plate, and decided it was time for the cold taste of sweet lemonade. He was going to put the fire out that was burning him on the inside. He had drank almost half of the lemonade in one gulp before he realized that it wasn't lemonade, but something completely different, spicy ginger beer. It was like pouring gasoline on a fire, and now it was all he could do to keep from passing out from the heat!! The heat had gone from being hot in a sauna, to jumping into a fire. There was no convenient pool of water to jump into!

The children excused themselves to get back to school, and he used that excuse to go the bathroom, and start drinking as much water as he could without embarrassing his hosts.

In the afternoon he went to look at the boat, and compiled lists of things that needed to be done to the boat.

Chapter Three

Rust Rot and more

Stan had studied the boat and eventually made lists of what was needed. Al's boat was a 26' long, fat, and comfortable boat (as best a 26' could be). The bottom had been scrubbed when it was pulled from the water, and the blue anti-fouling paint had obviously faded in the sunlight over the waiting years.

Frazer procured him a ladder so he could go topside. The keys that Al gave him opened the lock on the hatch and he realized when he descended into the darkened hull, time had deteriorated the boat. It was a fiberglass hull, but the deck was plywood with fiberglass over the top. The entire deck leaked on top and rotted underneath. Water intrusion had started with a small crack; a dropped anchor here, a winch handle there, or any heavy object falling on the fiberglass. As the water steamed in the sun, it cracked the fiberglass; more water entered and rotted more plywood. If someone stepped on the deck the weakened deck sagged and cracked some more. Water had leaked in, and there was water in the bilge, up to the level of the sink overboard drain. Al mentioned he had purposefully disconnected the drain at the hull fitting "just in case". Al in his wildest dreams could not imagine water getting into a boat sitting on the ground, with the hatches shut. The water at least could not get to a higher level.

The water had permeated everything. The mattress smelled, the wood smelled, and the whole boat said - rot. He realized that Al was right again, and he would have to spend "a month" fixing her up before putting her into the water. It was actually going to take much longer than that. Much longer.

Without much ado he began to open every window, and hatch and bail out the water. That had to be done by hand, as the hand bilge pumped was inoperative as the seals had rotted away. He stood in the hatchway and lifted buckets of water into the self-draining cockpit. To get the smell out of the boat, he had to take the mattresses out of the boat. They were all single berth mattresses, but water logged and mushy. They tore rather easily in his hands. Working up a major sweat he got the mattresses out of the boat and deposited them out in the blazing sun, and anything else he could lay his hands on. Two days later he would finally just throw them away. But for now he was trying to save everything he could, if it was salvageable at all.

Stan hit the bucket against the wood holding up the sink, and the framing had broken rather easily. With his hands he tore out most of the rest of the sink cabinet. Rot can weaken even the strongest structure. Fortunately the bulkheads were foam cored fiberglass, sealed pretty tight and therefore didn't rot. However, Stan began to suspect everything that was wooden on the boat had insidious rot. The whole boat smelled of must and mildew. There were mold spots all over the boat.

The plywood directly under the mattresses was tainted here and there with rot; the supporting structure was in need of replacement. The more rot he found, the more his spirit's sank. Each discovery spelled more work before he could begin "the dream". He was so busy inside sorting things out, that he was surprised when rain fell out of a sunny sky. What was already on deck to dry got soaked again. He also found out why there was so much water in the boat. Good thing Al had left the drain hose disconnected and the outlet valve open. The deck leaked. Not in one place, but many places. Not wanting to leave gaping holes, Stan began exploratory surgery and realized the whole deck and cabin house was either a sieve or a sponge. No wonder he encountered a dank smell when he opened the hatch.

By the time the afternoon sun began to beat on the boat he realized they had to rig a shade, or work would be impossible. It was like working in a sauna. With a lack of air flow down below, and the high humidity inside the boat, it felt like a steam bath. Before he got started very far, he felt like he needed a break. He climbed out of the boat and found he was wet completely from head to foot. What sweat had not wet, standing in water, and bailing and spilling water that splashed all over him. He went across the street and down a couple of buildings and entered a small rum shop. It had cold Coca Cola but no Pepsi. He knew he would have to find a way to get his preferred drink.

Stan went and talked with Frazer about getting wood and screws and whatever for the boat. That was going to constitute a trip into town, so he was going to have to close up the boat for the day. Instead, he climbed back inside the smelly dungeon and continued bailing and sorting what he could. He only quit when Frazer called him to go home. He locked up *Susan* and climbed down, realizing he would have a lot of work to do. Where the water had receded, there was a green slime stuck to everything.

Finally the sun went down over the horizon and the temperature and humidity began to cool. The sun near the equator does not give a lasting evening sky. Once the sun is below the horizon, it is dark within a half hour.

Later in the evening they went back to the airport to claim his luggage. While late, it was intact with nothing missing. He was thankful that he had come all this way and had everything to set to work.

He went to bed early that night.

Early Morning

He found by 5 AM it was useless to try and sleep. The neighbor's dog had gotten into at least two fights, the local rooster population was up and scratching about, and the neighbors were outside yelling about something. He later found out that the neighbors always yelled about something, every morning. He could not understand what they were yelling about, but he could always understand when they used the nasty word that began with the letter F. Later the neighbors bought a radio and he wasn't sure which was worse anymore;

to hear them argue or the music blaring very loudly. Generally he could hear both. They actually set the radio in the window, facing his bedroom window, and it was turned up loud. When you can feel the windows vibrate, you know it is loud.

By 5:30 the sun was streaming into the window and he elected to get up.

Even though he had showered before going to bed, he already felt sticky and clammy after a night in the hot humid air. He took another shower just to get awake and feel better.

He opted to go into town and eat a leisurely breakfast and check out the stores. Some of it would be window shopping, some of it would be to price wood and screws so he could begin work. He now realized it would be a major rebuilding project.

Frazier had told him about the public transport system, and a look at a map, he thought he could go into town and get back without getting lost. He politely declined Mrs. Frazier's offer for breakfast, and got an early ride into the capital. The visit to town yesterday was a help. He knew were KFC was, and he knew where the bank was located.

Van Ride

This was a complete immersion into Vincy culture; to stand out by the street and wait for a van headed to town. He was surprised when in less than five minutes he was on his way to town. An eighteen passenger van would cram in close to 22 people. A van would be called a bus, so would a regular bus, so would a truck with an open back with seats and a roof. Anything that moved was called a transport. Each van had to have a licensed conductor. His job was to insure that everybody could get in. What would have been almost comfortable for three people across in a row, he would squeeze four, and if they were skinny enough or children, there would be five or six. Then after there was no more room, he would stand and slide the door shut.

Stan was crammed in between a man on one side and a woman on the other. He definitely could enjoy the cushion on her side, but the man was bony on the other side, and every corner found the man's bones digging into his pelvis. Fortunately the van trip was less than half an hour. As the van made more money, making more trips, it was like a thrill ride at six flags over Georgia. But there were no seat belts, and no bar to lock you in. Turning a corner was an art in itself. Sometimes Stan could just use his feet and legs to brace himself, other times he had to grab the back of the seat to keep from falling into the person next to him. Later, he found that if he sat back and crammed in shoulder to shoulder, there was no room to move, and he would be held in place on the curves.

Shutting van doors was an art in itself. There was a great social awareness that you never, ever slam a car/van door. It would be ever so gently pulled up tight, and then one last pull to gently shut the door. Van doors never fell off track, or doors off their hinges.

Once inside the "Better than Six Flags over Georgia" ride began. The music was turned up to an ear splitting level. If you sat on the back row you would put your feet down by the speakers under the seat, and you could actually feel the rhythm. Stan also noticed that his pant legs were moving with the music. Speaking was not attempted in these kinds of conditions. For his first couple of trips, the fact that he couldn't understand the song's lyrics was a great blessing. Later he would find out just how nasty some of the songs could be. The choice of music, for the most part, was not "Caribbean style", but gangster rap from the U.S., so much for local culture.

The fare was definitely economical. He could get into town for less than 50 cents. However, evidently to pick as many people up during the rush hour traffic would call for as many trips as possible, or to beat the other vans to the bus stops and get the waiting fares. The only way to do that was - speed. Every turn you would hear the squeal of tires. Packed as they were, they were aware of the whole row leaning as they rounded the corners. Even though he thought this death defying trip was scary enough, he found out that the bus stops didn't mean where the buses were suppose to stop. They would stop anywhere, anytime, without any signals. The roads were very narrow, and a van almost blocked the road when he stopped. They must have some sort of way to signal what they were going to do, and a bus that was overtaking would not hesitate to pass a stopped van, and just get back in line before meeting an oncoming van. The blind corners were always interesting. Stan could never figure out how anyone could know that no one was coming - and yet the van would pull around a stopped van in the corners. Both vans would not know if there was an oncoming van. Oh, in this country they drove on the left side of the road, and that made for some interesting thoughts for the foreign travelers.

The only way he finally learned to relax was this was "business as usual" for the Vincies. The other passengers didn't seem to mind the music or the speed. When he found out that the government charged a 110% duty on vehicles and how expensive they really were, he realized that the van driver's really didn't drive with a death wish. They had far more to lose than he did. They were just trying to make the next van payments - and of course for some reason the insurance rates were very high also.

Breakfast and the Bank

Breakfast at the Bounty was "almost" American style of eggs. There was a flavoring on the eggs he couldn't quite place, but it seemed to come from something that looked like ketchup. The side dishes were Vincy; plantain, and fried hot dog. The cocoa was good.

A tour of the few hardware stores assured him that Al was right; bring your tools with you and use a transformer. Almost any power tool that ran on the 220 volt system used in St. Vincent cost more than four times its American equal.

He went to the bank to cash some cashier's checks. There was no queue; no standing in a line that snaked around the bank, and the next person in that line went to the next available teller. You just pick a teller and crowded in, just jam up to the counter and try to get the clerk's attention.

You hope that someone in front of you didn't have a commercial account and would dump out of a bag, a pile of coins. They lacked any coin rolls, and most people did not count their money before arriving. There were no machines that separated coins. No machines to count coins. People just dumped the bag out and began sorting a pile of coins. It could take awhile standing in line, while coins were sorted and counted. Stan stood in line for about an hour. They had fans, but no air conditioning. Between the regular temperature and body heat, Stan was very warm when he finally got waited on.

As he came up to the teller, a lady who was about 6' something and 330 pounds or so, crowded up behind him, pinning him to the counter in front of the teller. She handed some papers over the top of him. Someone walking behind the clerk began talking to her and the clerk. The three began sorting the papers that she had. For him, all he could do was stay there, helplessly pinned between the counter and the fat lady. For Stan he might as well be a WWE wrestler. While not pinned to the mat, he was pinned between the lady and the counter. This was an embarrassing situation, but he wasn't the one doing the pushing – she was. And he was stuck right there. The teller acted as though Stan did not exist and took her papers and did whatever it was she wanted done. When she got her business taken care of, which he had no understanding of the conversation (dialect again), she moved away and let him breathe and be waited on. That's when he found out he was in the wrong line!

Fortunately the next line was much shorter. Since he was going to open a foreign checking account, he was told to go to a different part of the bank to fill out the forms. They waited on him shortly after his arrival. He opened a checking account and deposited some cash, some traveler's checks and a check that Al had given them to use on "expenses". He was glad that E.C. dollars were counted in a decimal system. He was told that his check from the states would be on hold for forty days before they could give credit to his account. He felt uncomfortable carrying around as much cash as they were going to give him. He couldn't wait forty days, he needed E.C. money today. So Stan converted his traveler's checks to E.C. currency.

He made a note to tell Marcy bring a lot more Travelers Checks. One U.S. dollar bought $2.67 E.C. It made you feel rich. However, they would find that normal things, like food, were about 30% more than in the states, and other things like plywood, cars, computers, and other select items were off the scale in cost comparison. He felt like if he stayed long enough he could have set up a business.

Again, the experience of Al's was helpful. He had said there was only one supplier of fiberglass on the island, and he found that to be true. There was also very limited supply of anything found in the normal marine warehouses in the states. He was thankful for everything he had brought with him, and for a shipment of stuff that Al would send to arrive later.

Stores

Fortunately all vans stopped at "Little Tokyo" which was next door to Corea's Lumber and Trading. Stan went to order some plywood and found out that they operated on a different system from the United States. He was warned by Al not to think of this country as a small America, that it was really and truly different. It was.

Stan had to stand in line before he could order his wood. There was a little Plexiglas window separating him from the clerk, with a little round hole to speak through, and he could feel the "air con" (air conditioner) blowing out. He stood as close to the hole as he could, to get as much coldness as possible. He tried to order the wood and the lady said that they didn't have what he wanted. He had to go check with the man on the floor as to size and type of wood, and then come back and make his order. So after wandering around for awhile, he found a Mr. Browne who took him through the racks of wood, helping him in his selection of wood. There would be no exotic teak decks, nor cherry trim below. All they had was strictly exterior plywood and yellow pitch pine boards. And he was going to have to cut and plane every bit of it to get the size he needed. Pitch pine came in treated or untreated and rough or dressed (smoothed) and that was it. No other options.

Stan went back to the counter to place his order of wood. He was told he had to go in another line to pay for the wood. After paying for the wood he took the receipt back to the man in charge. Delivery was going to take several days, unless he wanted to pay a pickup truck driver who would gladly take his order to where ever he wanted, for a price. Not many choices here.

He barely got back by 4 PM and Frazer was waiting for him so he could close up the gate. So after off loading the wood he found out that the fare from town to the marina did not include the tip for the driver, or his helper. So their delivery price was much more than he expected, but it seemed cheaper than renting a vehicle. He just made a note to make as few trips as possible, and to be sure and order ahead of when he would need the wood.

Fishing Trip

One day when Stan got home early after work, Frazer announced that he was going fishing and taking his two oldest children, Estelita 9, and Julitha 13. Both were honor students in school, and very untypical Vincies. Estelita played the piano and Julitha played both the piano and the violin. They played classical music, not Calypso or Reggae. They were very respectful to their parents, and always answered questions with "Yes mam, or No mam" or "Yes sir", and "No sir". They both looked like their mother, and looked after their younger sibling. Julitha at thirteen was taller than Stan, and sometimes liked to just come up and stand next to him so she could look down at him. Not always perfect, as they pushed the envelope of what they could do and what they couldn't do. Both were always asking Stan and Marcy what it was like to live in the United States. Frazer asked if Stan wanted to go fishing with them.

So when the homework was put away, and Stan had changed into some non fiberglass itching, non stinking dirty clothes they all piled into the car. They stopped at a shop and Frazer bought each a Pepsi. They sat there in the car and drank them, and swapped jokes and fishing stories. The children were wide-eyed in the back seat unable to tell which was a true story and which was made up, but enjoying the whole conversation.

Stan knew better than to throw his Pepsi can out the window when he was finished, but he didn't exactly know what to do with it when he was done. Frazer informed him to save his can. They drove up a distance from the shop, up on the windward side of the island. When they got out and walked to the beach there was a hulk of a ship about 150 feet long. Its bow was jammed up on the shore and the stern was out beyond the breakers.

The tide was not very high, which is why Frazer chose this time to come. It helped greatly in getting to the ladder dangling off the front of the ship. But later when the tide was high, getting off the ship, it would provide a challenge of staying dry at the same time. On a second trip, Stan found out the tide came much higher on the beach, and it would be very difficult to get on the ship.

The waves churned at the shore leaving a phosphorus glow as they crashed on the beach. The moon was about half full giving a surreal light on the scene about to transpire. Stan hadn't noticed any rods and reels that Frazer brought, nor was he sure of what was going to be used for bait. Frazer and the children got out of the car and went around the beach overturning stones and in short order had filled a can with small crabs. Frazer retrieved a 100lb flour sack from the car, in which he put all the Pepsi cans. Stan noticed the sack that Frazer was carrying, but did not see any fishing rods. Stan was wondering how they were going to fish without any rod and reels. He was surprised at how easy it was to get bait off the beach so easily.

Then Frazer announced the difficult part. They were to run out on the beach and there was a ladder hanging from the front of the ship. They were to jump up and catch the ladder and start climbing. If they timed it right, they would get on the ship without difficulty, and without getting wet. If they were slow, or timed it wrong, well, they were going to get wet. Frazer had tucked all the empty Pepsi cans into the bag, along with the jar of crabs. He encouraged his children when to run for the ladder. Stan was a little amazed how deftly the children got on the ladder and began climbing without difficulty. They timed the waves, and made it look so easy. He wasn't so sure he would do as well. He was to learn later Frazer had brought the children here before, many times, and they had a practiced during the day when it didn't look so dark and scary.

The oldest child was almost to the top, the next was about half way up when Frazer said, "It is your turn." Not one word of encouragement, nor any clue as when to run for the ladder. Later he found out Frazer had told his children, "We shall see how Stan does in the dark, in the surf, and will he really climb a ladder up to a darkened ship? He might be real afraid you know. But, you won't be. So watch him and maybe you can laugh when he gets all wet."

Stan tried to time the waves, but ended up only on the first rung of the ladder when the wave hit. He hung on, and it only soaked him about half way up his leg. Being dressed for fishing, he had on tennis shoes and being somewhat new to the island, he also had on socks. Both were now sopping wet. He wore long pants and a shirt, but only the bottom part of his pants got wet. He climbed up the swinging ladder, to escape the water. By the time he looked up the children had already vanished from the darkened bow. But, if he had looked up from the beginning he would have seen four eyes staring intently over the bow waiting for him to get really soaked. It didn't happen, and they took off for the stern of the ship to check things out. A few minutes later the entire group was standing on the bow looking down on the crashing surf.

Frazer had a flashlight, but only turned it on when Stan approached an obstacle or set of steps on the boat. They worked their way to the back of the ship, and now Stan realized that this was a great fishing pier. The boat was steady underfoot, though you could feel a slight shake every time a wave came by. The stern was beyond the surf, and gave them clear water underneath.

At the stern, Frazer emptied out the bag, and there were no fishing rods. Each person was given an empty Pepsi can. Nylon line from a big spool was rolled unto each can. Near the end of the line a small piece of cork was attached then some stone was tied on for a sinker, and then a hook was tied on the end. While Stan was admiring the efficiency of the operation, he was dubious to the results. How were they going to get the line out far enough to not get washed back into the ship?

Frazer's children had done this before and with quiet efficiency spread out around the stern of the ship, giving each other plenty of room. Stan was still wondering what to do next after Frazer attached part of a crab that he had caught unto the hook. Frazer then baited his own hook and proceeded to give Stan a lesson in fishing that he had never seen before.

He stepped over to the side of the ship and began to swing the bait, hook, stone and cork in an ever widening circle, letting out fishing line as needed. Then when it all had a good amount of speed, like a bolo he let the line fly. He simply pointed his can that he held in the other hand, and let the line reel off, as the hook and everything disappeared into the darkness. Stan stepped over the rail and noticed when it splashed down, that it was well clear of the stern.

Now that he had seen the method of fishing, he stepped up to give it a try. Actually it was as easy as Frazer made it look. His hook had barely hit the water, when Estelita pulled in a fish, a small tuna about a foot and a half long. He thought tuna was only to be caught on the open sea, and with the use of nets or long line. He couldn't believe they had caught one so close to shore. Then another fish was caught, then he got one, and it just seemed to be a cycle that everyone was catching a fish. Sometimes Frazer was helping his children make the final pull of the fish up to the deck, as it had to be done quickly so the fish did not get away. They soon had a pile of fish flopping wildly on the deck.

Time seemed to not matter, but as they were enjoying themselves they became aware the moon had quit shining and a low level cloud was approaching. Frazer went around and scooped all the fish up and put them in the bag, along with, bait, line and anything else off the deck of the boat and finally had each person roll up his line back on the Pepsi can.

By then the first drops were beginning to fall. Frazer quickly got everybody to the bridge of the ship. There they stood inside the bridge while a tropical squall drenched the landscape. Stan was wondering now what they were going to do. It was pouring rain, and they had to go to the bow of the ship and go down the ladder. While he was getting nervous, the children were playing captain and spinning the steering wheel and giving commands as though the ship was still alive and going over the waves. While it seemed much longer, in about fifteen minutes, the storm had pretty well abated and Frazer made comment about the next row of clouds approaching. They had caught fish, and it would be a good idea to leave while it was still fun and an adventure, and not an endurance contest.

Quickly they all moved to the bow and hurriedly climbed down the ladder, children first. Stan for some reason didn't think about all that was going on, and in hopes of getting to the car before the next rain cloud came, forgot about the waves. He got to the bottom of the ladder and dropped on the sand, with just a little water on the top rushing across the top of the sand. In the hour or so they had spent fishing, the tide had come in, the storm that had just past had kicked up the waves a little higher, and before Stan could take a step, a wave came and rolled him over. He came out up higher on the beach with two children looking at him and really laughing. Frazer who saw it too, was also laughing. Frazer, like the children, timed the waves so that just his feet got wet. He did not have on shoes, and with short pants, he did not worry about getting salt water in his car.

The fish were in the same bag with all the fishing gear and were tossed into the trunk and they all headed home. Some of the fish were given to family and friends. Some of the fish were good for several meals, but the memory was something that would last a lifetime.

Chapter Four

Customs

Frazer informed Stan that the shippers had called and his box of tools and parts were at the customs warehouse, and he needed to go and collect the box. They had a discussion as to where that was located, and Stan felt like he could handle it on his own. He would hire a pickup truck to bring the stuff to the marina.

Stan went to customs to claim them. It was in a hot sweaty place, with all kinds of people milling around. Stan didn't have much of a clue what to do, and finally when he got someone's eye that seemed to be working there; he asked how to get his box. They asked him where the forms were that he was supposed to bring with him. He didn't have any papers and no clue as to where those forms would be. Then the customs guy asked him who the shipper was that called the house and said his box had arrived. He hadn't answered the phone and had no clue. They told him without the proper paper work, he couldn't get the box.

In those days there were few cell phones, and Stan didn't have one. He went back outside, walked five blocks up to the phone company, borrowed a phone book long enough to get Howard's Marine phone number and call Al and ask him who had called the house. Al had not answered the phone, and didn't know. He told Stan to call him back in 4 minutes, while he called his wife and asked her if she remembered. Stan stood in place to reserve his phone. The others phones were in use and people were in line. Stan even faked a phone call to keep the phone under his control. After standing in the sun reserving the outside phone so he could use it, with sweat pouring down his face, he called Frazer again and was told to check with International Shippers.

Looking in the phone book he found the listing for International Shippers. It only gave a street address, and he didn't know where that was. Town was basically two long streets; both were one way, going in opposite directions. One street was on the ocean side, and the other towards the mountain side. There was a street between, called Middle Street. It was very narrow and over run with vendors and most cars didn't even consider going through Middle Street. He asked for directions and had a four block walk to the International Shippers.

When Stan walked into International Shippers he just wanted to sit down and enjoy the air conditioning that most stores did not have. A tall cold drink would have helped, but, he just wanted to get through. A quick look found no chairs for prospective customers, a well worn wooden counter top between the customer and the office. It looked like a controlled explosion with some cabinets and file drawers, a couple of desks and all stacked with manila folders bulging with papers. There was an overhead fan that looked like it belonged to some early settlers with cobwebs and dust and rust visible from his point of view. It sat there uselessly, not a single blade looking like it had been used in years. It seems as if no office had anything more than a manual typewriter in those days. The internet was unknown and computers few and far between.

The lone lady in the room seem occupied with whatever it was she was doing and ignored him as though he was invisible. After a few minutes of waiting around he said, "I have come to pick up the paper work for a box that was shipped to me, Stanley Kerry."

Without a verbal reply the lady began sorting through a pile of papers on a center desk. He wasn't sure if she was really looking for his papers, or just a continuation of whatever it was when walked in.

"We have no paper work for you." She finally said.

Now Stan was stumped. How could he get his stuff? "But you called and said my box had arrived."

"Are you sure it was us? Maybe it was International Islands Shippers"

"No, I am not sure, so where are they"

"Down the street three blocks on the right."

So, Stan headed down Middle Street again, trying to hug the side where there was still some shade left. Later in the day Middle Street would be a fiery canyon as the sun stood overhead without any protection. The heat would radiate from the ground and off the walls. It was as if he was living a Lois La'mour western where the main character is out of water, out of food, out of energy, and everybody was out to get him. He had to will one foot in front of the other, as he automatically began to try to find shade. Where there were places he could walk in the shade, that is what he did. Three more blocks and he was beginning to wonder if he would ever get the job done. The sun was hot, and he was sweating. He was thirsty but did not stop in a store to get a drink.

Stan finally found International Islands Shippers and their office was opposite of the one he had just left. Its' only rusty fan was working, and they had no air conditioner. Since the lady behind the counter greeted him when he walked in he at least felt they just might be serious about customer service. They had the papers ready to hand to him, he had to hand them money for shipping and handling. Then they sent him back to customs. Four blocks in the direction he had just come!

At the customs shed the usual confusion was still going on, and he finally found an agent, and showed him the papers. He was told that he now had to get stamps for the paper.

"Stamps? What kind of stamps"

"Postage stamps."

"Postage stamps?"

"Remember the U.S. fought a war, about taxes? They were against the postage stamp act. We still have it."

"Where do I get them?"

The customs officer looked at him with a rather condescending smile, "At the post office. You need a $20 stamp." The customs officer was thinking, "isn't that obvious that you buy postage stamps at the post office."

To get to the post office, Stan had a five block walk back in the general direction he had already come. With sweat running down the middle of his back like a fast flowing river Stan got to the post office where he could purchased a $20 stamp. That was after standing in line for a twenty minute wait.

Standing in line always bothered Stan, especially when people cut in front of him. There were variants of that. People came in and recognized someone near the front of the line and handed them money to buy stamps for them, and then they would go and sit down while the other person would now take more time with the teller buying for two people. Sometimes they just cut in front. Other times they had already come, stood for awhile, and then told the person in front of them and in back of them to remember they would return. Some would sit down and watch the line snake around the queue. Others would actually leave and do something else, and upon return, get back in line behind the person they left.

The worst variable was that the post office, as well as the bank was a place to pay bills. So some old lady with a wad of money would pay her light bill, her phone bill, her cable TV bill, her cell phone bill, and water bill. Each bill had to be receipted for in triplicate. The stamp lady would take out a receipt book, place two pieces of carbon paper in the appropriate places, and fill each bill methodically by hand. Each bill had a different receipt book. Each receipt had to be stamped and initialed by the postage clerk. Of course if the customer was paying for two people, it would take twice as long before she would be finished. All that time – and she had never purchased a stamp!!

The next customer would step up to be waited on, and the scenario would repeat itself.

Stan just wanted one stamp so he could leave. It drove him crazy to watch all this going on. He found that many of the people in front of him were not there at the Post Office to buy stamps, but to pay bills.

Later he would find this same system in the bank. The clerk had no calculators, and he watched tellers count money and add on their fingers, or write it on paper and add or subtract. It just seemed to take forever. The whole thing went on while the ceiling fans were not cooling, and sweat continued to pour down Stan's back.

With a five block walk back. He arrived back at customs as they closed for lunch!

He decided to get lunch at Kentucky Fried Chicken which was SIX more blocks away from the customs house. It was the only American franchise on the island, and he knew they had air-conditioning. He was so ready for that. He arrived and had to stand in a hot sweaty line. The A/C had failed, and the temperature inside had risen and the sweat kept coming. The fans they brought in only stirred hot air. He didn't know what else to do, so he bought his two piece chicken dinner and ate by himself at a table. There were no refills on the drinks, unless he stood in line again, and paid for the second one. That was one thing he wasn't ready to do. He was hot and just wanted to get out of the place. He made a note that the next time he wouldn't stay if the A/C wasn't working. He would also order two drinks when he ordered lunch for himself, to save going for the refill.

By now the sun was high overhead, and there was very little shade. Kingstown, Saint Vincent is known as the city with arches. Many stores had built their second floors out over the sidewalk. The front of the store had some columns connected by arches and gave a very distinct look, different than the other islands in the Caribbean. It provided a nice shady walk way. But vendors had set up business on the sidewalks. They had army cots with items for sale, some had built tables, and some had built tables with shelves. The army cots were bad enough, but the tables were wider, and carried more goods. The sidewalk became a narrow crowded area, many times only one person wide. Walking in a hurry was impossible. Running into someone, literally, was normal. Stan walked in the street with the cars and other pedestrians frustrated with the vendors. Stan was walking in the sun now. No hiding from its blinding light. He found out very quickly that you can get badly sunburned if you were not careful. Luckily He had put on sun block before he left the house and he wore a hat. But now in the middle of the day, there was no getting away from the sun. It radiated heat up from the street; it bounced off the buildings, and shone brightly on top of his head. Sunglasses helped the eyes, the hat protected the head. But the heat was intense and Stan realized that sweat was a way of life, and you just got your clothes all wet from the sweat. The heat alone fatigued you and drew out your energy.

He got back to customs at 1:30, and had to get in line. Eventually they processed his box. The customs officer looked over the items, and declared he would have to pay $300 duty. That was more than it cost to ship them. He was so shocked, for used tools were hardly worth that. But there wasn't much to argue with and he had to pay. Since it was more money than he had on him, he had to go to the bank and withdraw some money. That took an hour wait in the bank. He was very fortunate as they closed the bank right after he got in line. He double checked his watch, they closed at 2pm. He had never heard of such a thing and there were no ATM machines to go to either. When he got back at customs at 3:00 they were locking up for the day!!

Another day, another trip this was getting to be unreal!!

He came back the next morning and thought he was finished with all the paper work, and could just pickup his box and go. But then, they noticed the UHF radio Al had sent down. They told him he would have to get a special license before they would release his items. They told him he would have to go to Communications to get the license. A six block walk up to the Communications Office and a half hour wait before he finally got to talk to someone about his radio.

They wanted to know the make, model, and serial number, which fortunately he had copied down before he left the customs area.

"We believe your information about the radio, but it is our policy to see the radio before giving a license" They said to him.

"But it is down at customs, and they won't release it unless you give me a permit to have it in St. Vincent."

"Sorry, but we must see the radio before we can give you a permit."

Could this get any worse? Stan had to walk six blocks back to customs to tell them that he had to have the radio in order for the Communications Department to see the radios before they would give him the license.

They told him he couldn't just walk out of customs with those radios, without that permit. They were not going to let his stuff go.

Stan had to walk the six blocks back to the Communications Department. The day was already heating up, and the sun was burning where he had gotten sunburn doing all the walking around yesterday. He was hot and getting hotter and he was sure it had nothing to do with the sun.

He went back up to the same office, waited another ½ hour before talking to the same man.

"I have to have the license to get my stuff out of customs."

"It is our policy to see the radio before granting a license."

"They won't let me walk with the radio unless I have the license." Stan was getting a little irate.

"You go tell them we will not grant the license unless we see the radio." The official stated.

Stan left, now he was really hot!! It was not the sun but he was just burning with anger!

Back at customs Stan again got into a discussion with the agent that became a little irritating to Stanley. They wouldn't let him walk out with the radio without the license. The people at Communications wouldn't give the license unless they see the radio. What nonsense!

At last there was a ray of hope when another customs agent came by and listened to the discussion. He called over a third man and handed him the radio.

"Take this radio and this man to Communication, and make sure he gets a permit. Return the radio to here." He said.

So the two walked back to Communications and they waited another ½ hour before the original official looked at the radio. You would think that he would really inspect it, and check to see if the serial numbers were right, etc. No. He just took it in his hand and set it on the desk. He punched a button on his phone and spoke into it.

"Bring the forms for UHF radios." Stan assumed the secretary was listening at the other end.

The secretary brought a form to him to sign. The official gave her the original paper Stan had given to him for the serial numbers, make and model. Stan and the man from customs were then told to go back and wait. So the customs man took the radio and disappeared with the radio, while Stan waited until the paper work was done. Before they would give him the permit, he had to pay $150.

That payment had to be made at the Treasury, four blocks away. Again, Stan walked the streets of Kingstown wondering what other surprises he had for the day. He returned with a receipt, and then they told him he had to have a stamp. A $20 postage stamp, which he would have to get at the Post Office, which just happened to be next to the Treasury building where he had just paid the $150! Why didn't they tell him that when he went to pay the bill?

Stan was really hot, and this time it had nothing to do with the sun. He knew showing how upset he was wouldn't help at all. Stan had to walk the four blocks to the Post Office, purchase a stamp and return to Communications. There they finally gave him his permit. He walked back to customs and they finally processed him through.

After two long days he finally had the tools he thought he would need for the job at hand. He was tired, had sunburn, and his feet hurt from all that walking on the concrete streets of Kingstown. He decided he was just too hot and tired to work any on *Susan* for the rest of the day.

Stan walked into a store and because they had a transformers in the window, and purchased a big enough transformer for all his tools. Later, he found that was an unwise move because he could have gotten one cheaper at another store, with a handle. But, with the mood Stan was in, he didn't care, he just wanted to get done and get home.

Spear Fishing

While People have used nets for years to fish, that was not Stan's thing. People used line and hooks, with or without poles. He did enjoy fishing off the stranded ship, but, Stan always liked the idea of going in the water, after the fish, with a spear gun. He could select what fish he really wanted, and at the same time gave the fish an opportunity to escape. He felt like it was a sporting thing to do.

One Saturday Frazer hung up the phone and asked Stan if he wanted to go fishing. So Stan quickly got his gear together and by the time he was finished two cars pulled into the driveway. They left enroute the leeward side of the island. In Layou they turned off following the main road, kept going straight and in a short order of time, ended up at a resort that had only one entrance. With towering cliffs, and steep hillside, they arrived at the resort and had to pay a minimal fee at the gate to enter the property.

They parked almost on the beach and the two cars began to unload. Stan climbed out and took off his shoes. He screwed together four two foot aluminum sections, to make a pole 8' tall. One end had surgical tubing attached in a loop; the other was the business end that had three prongs.

The pole spear worked very simply. As you hooked your hand through the surgical tubing, and slid your hand down the poll as far as you could lever it, your hand gripped the pole and you were then in a ready position. When the pole was released, the three stainless steel prongs sprung slightly open as the spear rushed through the water. When it hit a fish and stopped moving, the steel springs closed back together again, and trapped the fish so he couldn't escape.

Stan had used the spear gun, and a pole spear and a Hawaiian sling. The Hawaiian sling was much like a bow and arrow arrangement, without a wood bow. It was powered by surgical tubing. It was arranged so that a steel arrow was notched and fitted into the string that connected endings of the surgical tubing. The tubing laced around your hands and fingers, and you drew it back as you would a bow and arrow. You let it go, and the steel arrow flew to the target. There was no line attached to it as there is in a spear gun. You picked your target carefully, because you would have to chase the arrow where ever it went. Sometimes the arrow would go all the way through the fish, and it would swim away with a hole in its body.

The spear gun had the best long range, and it had the more power. It had a fid on the end that folded down over the spear and came up after the spear penetrated the fish. The other end of the spear was a line attached back to the spear gun. Some had two surgical tubings for power, and extremely large fish have been speared by the spear gun.

But, for the most part Stan preferred the pole spear. If there was a miss, many times the spear would stick in the ground. Stan would simply swim down the pole while sliding his hand into the surgical tubing. When he grabbed the pole, he was ready to fire. He would then pull the spear out of the ground.

Most fish seemed to jump when a shot missed them. They would go a few feet, and then turn sideways and look at Stan, as if to say, "What was that all about?" Stan would swim down the pole, hooking his hand in the surgical tubing, and when he got as far as he could, lock his hand around the pole and pull it out of the ground. He was now ready to fire the second shot. Generally the fish was still sideways looking at him. Many times the second shot was closer than the original shot. While a very unusual fishing weapon in St. Vincent, Stan felt it was the best choice for what they were doing.

So Stan had stepped out the car, removed his shoes, screwed the pole together and he was ready to go.

Frazer's friend, Watson, at 6'5", looked down at Stan. Watson had removed his street clothes and was standing in his bathing suit, with his spear gun in hand and studied Stan. He had realized that Stan was leaving his shirt and pants on, and had this strange looking weapon.

"You're kidding mon." Watson smirked.

"What do you mean by that?"

"Mon, you goin swimmin like dat? Wa yo bathing trunks?"

"I go in all the time like this, with pants and shirt."

"I neva seen dat before."

The conversation and the underwater hunting party headed to the ocean. Stan had sprayed the inside of his mask with a de-fogger spray so it wouldn't cloud up when he got in the water. The Vincies broke off some leaves and coated the inside of their masks to prevent, the same thing. Stan's spray was bought in the store for a couple of dollars. While what the Vincies did accomplished the same thing, it was free. Stan still had some learning to do.

Out in the ocean they were spearing in an area where the water just tapered out to a cliff. The edge of the cliff was probably about ¼ mile from the shore and it was probably about 50 feet down. In a boat, the water turned from brown near the edge, to green, and then a dark blue at the cliff edge. You could almost know the depth by the color of the water, without a fathometer. Brown, you get out and walk, green, it is shallow, and it depends on how much draft your boat draws. Dark blue was deep, safe water.

Spear fishing had to be done where the fish were, and where the hunter felt at home to go. Most were fishing in the 10-20 foot range. Stan would select his fish and when he was ready, jackknife on the surface and when he lifted his legs out of the water the weight drove him down. He could reach over 10 feet down very easily this way. If needed, Stan kicked with his feet. Sometimes he would dive straight down on the fish, other times he would slant in at 45 degrees and trail behind the fish. Most fish took shelter behind or under a rock. If they could find a cave they would go inside. Stan would make sure that he could hold his breath long enough so that when they stuck their head out to check on him, he could take his shot.

Anything beyond 12 feet Stan would have to hold his nose, and blow gently to equalize the pressure on his ears. Some never go that deep, because they cannot get the pressure equalized. Stan seemed to have no problem equalizing the pressure on his ears.

Frazer had shot at a large fish further out. He had missed another fish and the spear point had stuck in the coral. He could tug on the spear gun to get it dislodged, but the fid had deployed and it was stuck in the coral rock. When Stan noticed Frazer, he was standing almost vertical in the water, holding his snorkel so he could do so. Most snorkels fit comfortably on the side of the mask, where the swimmer can lay on the surface and stare straight down and breath without any problems. Standing vertically changes that angle. You have to hold the snorkel to get it above the water.

Watson's 6'3" frame was vertical in the water. He had on some large fins, and was barely touching the end of the spear gun. There was almost no current, and it was almost a straight line from the tip of the spear, stuck in the ground, to the butt of the gun. Later, Watson measured from the spear point to the end of the gun, and it was almost 40'. He figured the depth was at least 40-45' down.

Watson took a dive but, only reached about half way and came back to the surface.

Stan studied the situation for a moment, breathing deeply. He then jackknifed and headed for the bottom. He went to the point of the spear, and grabbed the spear. He jiggled it loose, and then turned towards the surface. He returned with no difficulty, and after that Watson, and no one else ever said, "You kidding mon."

Wallilabu anchorage

Chapter Five

Falling off the Boat

Stan sorted through a box and some barrels that were locked up in a giant shed. Stuff not stored on the boat; navigational charts, compasses, lights, pots, pans, sails and anything else of value or importance. That stuff seemed to fare better than what was left on the boat. Al had even taken all the standing stainless steel rigging off the mast and stored it in the box also. He would have to sort out which were backstays, and which was the forestay, and which were the sidestays. But unlike stuff left on the boat, this stuff was in good condition. Al had greased all the stainless steel parts and anything else he thought would corrode with time. Books and charts were in the barrels where no bugs could enter and they were as good as the day they were stored.

He talked to Frazer and he agreed to let him have the key to the front gate of the marina. Stan realized he needed to get there early and work before the sun came up enough to cook him. He would probably cease work in the afternoon and work again later as the sun began to go down.

He realized that the entire deck would be easier to replace than fix pieces of it. Working below decks would be somewhat easier with the deck removed as he rebuilt all the cabinets. Stan began with the crowbar and hammer to dismantle what he could. He was also going to have to order more wood. He was also going to have to stop into a cyber café and email Al what was going on, and that he would need more money. Al's rebuilding check was going to be spent rapidly. After all, a boat is defined as a hole in the water in which you pour money. This boat had a hole full of water in which you pour money. Al had seen their wood working abilities in the states, and was going to have to trust them for whatever they did to his boat.

Stan was an obsessive compulsive type who just wouldn't stop until a job was finished. They had flown all the way down here, they knew they would have a lot of work to do, and he wasn't going to quit until it was done and the boat was floating in the water, back in Miami. What he hadn't planned on was all the obstacles. The dream was becoming a nightmare. The adventure had become an endurance test. The excitement was gone and frustration poured in. The mountain was indeed a mountain. A background of plugging along and getting the job done was what kept him going.

Stan measured pieces and marked them before he ripped them out. They would be useful for patterns when he began replacing them The thing that kept going through his mind as the sweat dripped off his face, was he was glad the boat was only 26'. This could have been a real job had it been any larger.

Locals who came by kept offering their help, and he kept turning it down. But in the end he hired a man for a couple of days as they rigged the awning, and ripped things apart. They guts of the boat were soon lying on the ground around the perimeter of the boat. The deck had almost disintegrated with rot and had come out in pieces. Fortunately, Stan kept taking pictures. In the end they would have words with Al as to what was done to the boat, and pictures were good proof.

Stan rigged two tarps. The one that came with the boat was over the boat. He also rigged another over the side of the boat to give shade to one side of the boat where they could work on the ground. At one point in the heat of the day and dehydration, Stan stepped backward on the deck of *Susan* and stepped onto the side tarp. Maybe his mind thought the tarp was just an extension of the deck or that the canvas was sturdy and would hold him up. Maybe he was tired and just didn't think.

It gave way as though it didn't exist. Stan fell straight down for eight feet where he landed flat of his back! He narrowly missed the saw horse on the ground, which would have broken his back if he had hit it!! He lay there out of breath and unable to talk. His helper came over and grabbed him by the hand and tried to jerk him to his feet. Stan was not feeling anything because of the shock, but, screamed as best he could, and jerked his hand away.

"No. Let me lie here for awhile," screamed Stan.

His helper moved on to some other task as if every day people fell off boats unto the ground and wanted to lie there! After Stan could begin to breathe freely, he slowly got to his feet and checked himself out. Except for the memory of stepping into thin air, and falling, he had no marks, bruises, or broken bones to show for the experience. But, he was well aware that death had stalked him and narrowly missed.

After Marcy came the work began to go a little faster with the two of them. She could cut some things, hold things down, pass tools and parts. Her main job was procurement, while he did the physical work. They began making lists of what they needed to do, and what they needed to get the job done. Since the marina could give them a safe place to store things, they made as few trips to town as possible. It took a half hour in, and at least half hour back; just for transport time. Then shopping in stores without air conditioning, and having to walk several blocks to different business in the sun, generally left one more worn out at the end of the day instead of the one who worked all day on the boat. Then they discovered the price differences. An item at one store could be bought dollars cheaper at another store. If you bought all your lumber at one place, and then nails at another, you could save money. If not, you paid too high for something. Finally they decided the walk wasn't worth it, and to get on with repair work, they just adapted the policy, if you see it - buy it.

Days began to stretch into weeks, and they learned that they were in St. Vincent, a Caribbean island, and while they were looking at finishing the boat and cruising to the islands now was the time to see what they could see. In the beginning they worked from sun up until sundown. In the tropics that was a twelve hour day. As time drug on, they began working 40 hours a week instead of 60-70. They began to spend more time touring the island. So they began to see the tourist sites. After all, that is what they came for, to see the countries.

Zip Line

In the first week of Marcy being there, Frazer rigged a zip line across his back yard between the mango tree and the coconut tree. The kids loved it, and he could hear them yelling as they jumped out into space and hung on the pulley contraption that they rode down from the Mango tree to the coconut tree. The mango tree was uphill of the coconut tree so they had a good slide.

This was not a professional rig; there were no safety harness, or nets to catch you. Frazer had inherited the cable off a yacht that had been dismasted. The owner replaced the entire rig, and Frazer carried the cable home, and with some clamps, attached it to the tree. He made a pulley rig where the pulley rode on top of the cable, and two handles hung down to hang onto. You reached around the tree to grab the handles, and pushed out over the middle of nothing. You held on tight as you went downhill, ten to fifteen feet off the ground. It was an exhilarating ride and not for the faint of heart, or weak hands. You held on until your feet drug on the ground, and you tried to stop yourself before you hit the coconut tree at the bottom of the hill.

Stan had watched the kids enthusiastically enjoy the ride, and other kids from the neighborhood would come and play from time to time. It did look like fun, and he was here in the Caribbean to enjoy himself so he began to give it some thought; he would like to try it out. But, it seemed more of a kid thing, than what adults did, so for awhile he didn't indulge himself.

But one day when he came in from work, while hot and sweaty, he was not really exhausted, and Estelita challenged him to give it a try. So he decided that he would.

Climbing the tree was more formidable than he would like to admit. He hadn't climbed trees even as a kid, as best he could remember. He wasn't even sure he liked heights, though he wasn't scared of the view once on top. They had nailed some steps in the side of the tree, which helped as he climbed up.

They had a small line that looped over the handle of the trolley, and they used this to walk the trolley back up the hill and position it for the next rider. He took a hold of one handle and they flicked the line off the other handle and he was all set. He was somewhere between ten and fifteen feet off the ground, his two feet on the last ladder rung, right hand on the trolley. Now came the hard part. He had to turn loose of the tree with his left hand, and reach across and grab the left trolley handle, which was the farthest handle from his position. He then had to twist his body, kick off with his feet and start this glorious ride to the bottom as he had seen the other kids do.

As he turned loose with the left hand and reached across… years later looking back he doesn't remember anything else.

His wife would fill in all the details. She saw him get both hands on the trolley and jump off the step with his feet. But, as he moved forward, the pulley evidently jumped the tracks and jammed. His body kept going forward and his body momentum forward was enough to make him turn loose when he began to flip. He did a complete flip in the air. He then fell about 10 feet and bounced when he hit the ground flat on his back.

On the ground he only remembers seeing them looking down at him and somebody saying, "Don't worry the ambulance is coming." Later he realized he was thinking "why would the ambulance come?" Stan doesn't remember the ride to the hospital. But, later when he woke up in the hospital, his entire body hurt.

At the hospital they found out they had to provide sheets and pillow.

He wore a temporary soft neck brace for about a week. The x-rays only showed one spur on his spinal column had fractured. It felt like every muscle in his neck and back had been pulled and strained very badly. He does remember the conversation with the doctor.

"I have a question for you." The doctor said.

"What is that?" Stan replied

"Why aren't you dead? Or, why aren't you paralyzed from the neck down?"

The best answer Stan could give was, "I came to St. Vincent to do a job, and I can't do that in a hospital bed or if I am dead."

By now he was beginning to have a dread of high places.

He fully recovered in a couple of weeks, with just some lingering soreness. But for the first few days he was glad that Marcy was a willing nurse, and would tend to his every whim. He was also very thankful, life had not ended.

Chapter Six

The Truck

Getting around the island posed a problem without your own vehicle. Stan was use to jumping in a car and going whenever, and wherever he felt like. If he wanted lunch, he drove home or to a restaurant, but now he had to wait for a van to take him to and from his destination. Many times they were coming by every five minutes but sometimes it was longer. ANY wait annoyed Stan to no end. A couple of times he borrowed Frazer's car, but realized that carrying sticky, dirty stuff was not appreciated by Frazer who kept an immaculate car. Frazer even washed his car every night. Later when a gallon of paint got loose, Stan was glad that it was in the back of the truck and not in the trunk of Frazer's car. It created quite a mess and dripped out the back of the bed of the truck. Vans even drove in the trail of paint thinking it was mud because of the color; but later found out that it was paint when it had already dried solidly to their vehicle.

There was an old truck that was on the side of the Frazier property that looked the opposite of his car. It was an American

Ford 250 eight cylinder truck that had more rust than steel. Somehow the tires were still holding it up. The bed had rusted away, but Frazier had made a wood floor. The floor inside was also gone, but the massive frame was still intact. Frazier just happened to make a comment, "The engine runs." From that day forward Stan eyed the truck with hopeful eyes. Finally the conversation turned to the truck and Stan offered to get it running, if he could use it. Frazier didn't have the time, and gladly offered it to Stan. Stan was glad for all the times his dad had made him work on the family car, and his own car when he first bought one.

It surely wasn't much in the way of looks. The bed had rusted away and had been replaced with the plywood bed. Seats were built on the sides, an improvement over the old truck. This posed the next problem, because people were always asking for a ride "to town".

The truck was painted a dull red. It helped disguise the rusted metal of the truck body, but it also disguised the dripping rust running from all the nails on the plywood seat arrangement.

Frazier had built a wooden frame over the top, and made an easy way to raise and lower heavy duty tarp down the sides to shield passengers from the rain. While not totally dry, it did prevent everyone from getting dripping wet.

The gas tank was only a plastic, five gallon boat engine tank. It worked OK, but with an eight cylinder engine, five gallons didn't take long to consume, nor did it take as much money to fill.

One day while driving down the street, the back window of the cab just fell out when they hit a bump. The sides of the window had finally rusted all the way through. Rust is so prevalent, that the banks would only give one and half year loan on a new vehicle. After that, the rust would be so bad; the vehicle was not worth very much.

The floor under the feet of the driver was rusted almost completely away. Whenever it rained, which happened often, water would spray up into the cabin. The joke was about it being a religious truck, because of the foot washing ceremony one went through when they hit a puddle. At high speed, everybody just got a complete shower.

One day when Stan was driving he wondered why the engine was so mistimed, that it coughed and sputtered so often. He pulled over to the side of the road and popped the hood open. As the sun had just set, it was already getting dark. Inside the hood, it was all lit up. A great fireworks display was going on under the hood. He watched all spark plug wires, and anything that carried high voltage, were grounding out all over the inside of the engine compartment. It was quite a show with electrical sparks everywhere. He couldn't see a particular pattern, and figured that salt spray had gotten inside the wires, and they were just going to short out no matter what he did. He just shut the hood and drove on with it kicking and missing.

Transportation was as simple as it comes. A vehicle was to get from point A to point B. Anything else was just extra. Reliability was more important than the latest sound system. That it would start without pushing, or using a jump start, was more important than the condition of the seats.

Fortunately speeds were slow. Clamps were carried so that when the ball joints gave way, and the wheels would point in different directions, you could jack up the truck and using the clamps re-attach the ball joints and carefully go on your way. Replacing the joints on Stan's truck was done by going to a junk yard and finding a similar vehicle, with what you hoped were good ball joints. They cut them free, turned the joints 180 degrees and welded them back together. Putting them on Stan's truck cured his ball joint problems

The police would stop you if one headlight was out. Once, Stanley was driving and passed a police car going in the opposite direction. Watching in the rear view mirror he saw the police turn around and head towards him. He knew they would stop him. He knew his low beam on the left side was out. He had it on low beam when they past each other. He flipped the headlights on bright and got out of the truck.

A polite "Good night" was not acknowledged by the officer as he kept on walking to the front of the truck. It was with surprise that the officer turned and found two headlights lit. He stated that when they had just passed, Stanley had only one headlight working. Stanley replied that maybe there was short circuit, and he would check it out in the morning. The officer seemed satisfied and drove away. Stanley drove home with lights on bright.

Stan always carried a flashlight for the truck, sometimes two. One time the headlights failed for no apparent reason, and in order to get home, he taped two flashlights up on the fenders and drove home.

Admiralty Bay with trimaran

The Tires

The tires on the truck were split rim, an unusual combination to Stanley. There was the usual rim, but a steel ring (round circle with a section missing) that fit snugly on the INSIDE of the regular rim. That split steel ring held the tire in place. It took some work to spread that steel ring apart enough to get it to fit over the regular rim.

There were only two places that would even work on those tires. The primary place was a shop that Stan was unaware if it even had a name. There was no sign out front. The owner was a very muscular young man, who used a sledge hammer to get that split ring over the steel rim. Stan watched as he poured sweat over that tire. Sweat was dripping off his head, hands and arms. It was a job he really didn't want for himself.

The second was a place called "Public Works". Many thought of that as it stated. The public could come and have done what they needed done. Sometimes Stan would take tires there.

Flats were common. Working in a boat yard, there were a fair amount of nails and screws lying around. The coral itself that was found all over the island, was sharp enough to cut a tire.

Not once was there a mention that this method was dangerous. Stanly watched several tires being repaired without any thought of safety. Later he was to notice in the States that sitting in a corner of most tire shops that catered to trucks or buses was a steel cage. That steel cage contained a tire until it had the tire inflated and hit on with a hammer to test that it was seated properly. If it wasn't, the split rim would come off in a split second, with tremendous force.

Embarrassed by the number of flats, and to avoid the expense of paying someone to work on his flat tires, Stan decided he could do the job himself. He had also been told by his primary tire repair place, to not bring a flat tire again! The man had decided the amount of sweat involved in getting the split ring over the steel rim, was not worth any amount of money.

That left Stan one day in Frazer's yard fixing the tire himself. He had a sledge hammer, he had a repair tool/kit for the tubeless tires, and he had an air compressor. The work that began in shade had turned to full exposure to the sun as the day progressed. He was dripping sweat and had puddles of water formed from the sweat off his body. He was finally ready to add air to the tire.

The tires said inflate to 60lbs but he was not sure what pressure his air compressor would produce. If Stan got it to seat properly, and get to 35-40 lbs he would just pump the rest by a regular, old fashion hand tire pump. The noise of the compressor was in his ears as he began inflating the tire. He was reaching across the tire to hold the compressor hose to the tire valve. Out of the corner of his eye he noticed that Frazer moved away from him and the tire. For reasons he does not yet comprehend, Stanley undid the connection between the compressor and the tire valve. He stepped back a couple of feet, and without warning the steel rim came loose off the tire, and in an explosion of air, the steel rim shot into the air.

To this day Stanley still has burned into his memory that steel rim above the coconut trees in a perfect circle. To this day, Stanley is absolutely positive, that had he not taken that step back, he would be dead. Death stalked in vain one more time.

Final end of the Truck

Later, when the boat was done and Stanley and Marcy finally left, Frazier took the truck to "Public Works" and gave it to them. Frazer took the battery home. They thought they were going to keep the truck on the road, but within a week discovered it was as Frazer had said, "It would be good for parts."

Driving Frazier's Car

When the steering wheel is on the right side of the car, and you grew up with it on the left, it is easy to make a fool of yourself. There must be a Chinese proverb somewhere about that.

Stan had actually gotten pretty good at adjusting to driving on the left side of the road. The truck was a left had drive, and all he had to do was stay close to the ditch and he would be on his side of the road. Frazer's car was right had drive and keeping in the left lane was "a little different." The biggest difference for Stan was inside of Frazer's car.

The shift was on the floor, but on the left side not the right. He kept trying to open the car door instead of shifting into second gear, or any gear for that matter. More than once Stan laughed at himself when he was trying to shift the gears and had his hands on the door handle. At least when your hand hit the door handle you knew you were not on the shift lever, and somehow he never accidently opened the door. It protected his ego to know that the people on the outside of the vehicle didn't know what he had done.

However the windshield washers and turn signal were mounted on the steering column, but on opposite sides from the American standard. More than once Stan went to turn on the signals, and instead squirted water over the windshield or turned the wipers on, embarrassing when the sun was clearly shining. Instead of signaling his intentions people would suddenly see his windshield wipers going across the windscreen.

Since he drove with the windows rolled up and the air conditioner on, he couldn't stick his hands out the windows and give directions as to where he was headed.

The most embarrassing moment though occurred when Stan forgot which side the steering wheel was located when entering the car. With a sidewalk audience watching his every move, or so it seemed, he carefully unlocked the left side to the car and got inside, and with key in hand looked for the ignition. There was none! Then he noticed that there was no steering wheel in front of him. Climbing over the center console and gear shifter didn't look like a good option with prying eyes staring at him through the windscreen. This was embarrassing.

He was sure they had seen this before and were waiting for him to get out of the car and go to the other side and unlock the door and get in on the right side. Then of course they would have a good laugh at this "crazy foreigner."

In a stroke of genius he laid the keys up on the dash and proceeded to open the glove box and slowly take out everything, shuffle through the papers, and eventually put everything back. He closed the glove box door, grabbed the keys and climbed out of the car. He noticed even more eyes were focused on him from the surrounding audience. He then proceeded to the "driver's side door" on the right side, and unlocked it and got in the car. After backing out of the parking place, he was so glad to get away from preying eyes that he didn't even look in the mirror as he drove away.

Spare Parts

One day when Frazer and Stanley were talking about cars and swapping stories, Frazer was impressed how Stan owned all kinds of vehicles, and Frazer could barely afford to buy a couple of vehicles in his lifetime. The idea that Stan, when he was growing up, bought his first vehicle for $200 and drove it for several years was beyond Frazer's comprehension. Frazer could not conceive of a car so cheap. SVG imposed a 110% duty on cars, and that included the value of the car and shipping added together to form the base when they assessed duty charges.

Stan could only nod when Frazer told him such things. He noticed most vehicles were kept running well past their "prime". Even though parts were assessed the same 110% duty tax, it was a lot cheaper than getting a newer vehicle. However there were times when Frazer said "you just had to go for the newer vehicle".

At one point Frazer bought a six year old Starlet, made by Toyota for $20,000. Stan had never seen one in the states, but they were here on the island. Stan was calculating the cost in his head, what that would be in the U.S. As the story continued, Stan came to roughly $7,000 U.S. and had to agree that is more than he had paid for a vehicle, ever. Frazer said it gave him excellent service, even though it looked like a shoe box with wheels. Getting in and out of the vehicle was not easy either, with him being so tall. Frazer purposed from then on, price would not be the only consideration in buying a vehicle. If he couldn't get in and out of the vehicle easily, he wouldn't buy it.

Frazer had driven it for almost 14 years. The air conditioner finally died and was not worth the cost to fix. The panels on the inside of the door were taken out so you could push the window up and down with your hands while you rolled the crank. To keep them up you then jammed a stick between the slot in the bottom of the door and the window channel. There were some serious rust spots, (despite two trips to have the body welded and cut on and body work done), it evidently was beginning to look like the truck Stan had used.

Finally Frazer had had enough of pouring oil into the vehicle on a regular basis. He couldn't always catch all the oil that dripped out from underneath when he parked it. Not having the time to work on it, he turned it over to a mechanic who was to find the source of the oil well that was coming from under the car.

A couple of days later, the mechanic presented him with a rubber "O" ring that was about 1" across, and told him he needed a new one. This is the seal that holds the oil pump on the car engine. Mechanics in St. Vincent did not stock parts; neither did they spend their time going all over town to find it. The owner of the vehicle was expected to do that, so Frazer began his hunt for the part. The simple places where they sold such commodities turned up nothing. One of the newest stores was U.S. based with NAPA part numbers. His Toyota Starlets didn't even show up on their parts list. Even if they had a part, it was probably for left handed drive cars, and wouldn't fit the right handed drive vehicle that Frazer drove.

He had even gone to the Toyota Dealership where he bought the car. They looked in their micro film machine and came right out with a part announcing this was what he needed. He had the old one in his hand, and when comparing the two it was obvious they were different sized. They couldn't figure out how there was a difference nor how they could order one like his. Because this was the only Toyota dealership on the island, this was not good news.

Some trips to different junk yards didn't turn up anything. Frazer would even knock on doors that had a similar car parked in the yard. That too proved fruitless. At this point Frazer really didn't have any hope.

He found an outfit working out of a store front with very few parts on hand. They assured him they had someone going to Trinidad and they would get him the part. They needed his old part to take with them to compare with a new one. Handing the part over, knowing it was going to Trinidad, was hard. If the part happened to be misplaced, then what would he compare things to? He had a very good working knowledge of the island stores; he knew there were not any options left. He reluctantly handed it over.

Two weeks later they called to say they hadn't found the part! He was now stuck. He had no further options that he knew of. He asked for the part back. They told him to come in three weeks to collect it when the messenger returned. He hung up the phone not knowing what to do.

Frazer and his wife talked it over and decided that with a growing family, it was time to get a van. By emptying their checking and savings account they could maybe buy one. They proceeded to go shopping and finally decided on an eight passenger van. It had all the modern conveniences; power windows, power locks, and air conditioning that wasn't going to be used much by them. While the van was 6 years old, it was 26 years newer than their car. Maybe they could sell their car for parts and get back some of their savings account. But financially it was going to be a major expenditure for them.

They bought the van and had enjoyed it for about a week, when they received a phone call from the store informing them that they had found their part in Trinidad. When they picked it up, it was $5.00 E.C., which Stan interpreted as $2.00 U.S.

"So," said Stan, "for a lack of a $5.00 part you bought a $33,000 van?"

"We had been without a vehicle for almost 6 months, and decided that was the best decision."

"Was it?" queried Stan.

"Well, as soon as we got the van we found out that people wanted a ride here and there. If you didn't give them a ride, for free especially, you were a bad guy." Frazer was just stating the facts.

"The truck you are driving is worse. People always needed stuff moved here and there – and if you don't do it when they wanted, for free, you were a bad guy again. The car seems to be the best thing to remain friends with neighbors and relatives." Frazer concluded.

Chapter Seven

Church service – Funeral Service

Frazer was insistent they shouldn't work on Sunday and he invited them to church. They had obtained a good case of sunburn, and their office jobs had not prepared them for constant work in the physical realm of every day. Their bodies needed a rest and they decided this was as good a time as any to sample the local culture. They expected when they showed up on a boat, in an exotic port, they would visit the land. Why not see the same sights they would try to see as if they were not on a boat? Why not start now?

So they put on the best set of clothes they had packed and went to church. Both put on the longest pair of shorts in their possession. Stan had only one pair of long pants. He had worn them to work, and now they were all stained with epoxy. So he could not wear what he thought would be appropriate, but this was the Caribbean, and put on a pair of shorts. Marcy didn't own a skirt, and had left all long pants in cold America. Marcy and Stan's clothes were all cotton, and needed pressing. They didn't have an iron, and didn't think of asking Fraser's for one.

Stan wore his open sandals, and Marcy had on her best pair of sneakers. Neither wore socks.

Nobody commented they were not properly dressed, but maybe that was because they definitely looked like tourists and weren't expected to dress as everybody else. They were the only white people in the congregation. They took noticed how the other people looked like "Esther's pet mule". The men were dressed in white, long sleeve shirts, with black suits. Black socks and black shoes, and the black ties were the topping on the cake. Some men had hats. The ladies all wore hats, and the dresses were out of no catalogue they had ever seen. Super dressed, they wore dresses like worn at weddings or special state functions. However, the colors and color combinations were different to say the least. Sometimes there seemed to be color co-ordination. Other times, they just clashed. Nobody seemed to mind.

It was amazing to them to see all that material that made up the dresses. However, with all that cloth, the ladies seemed to be pouring out the top of their dresses; exposing a significant upper part of their body. Didn't they think this was more improper than wearing shorts? The word "pouring" came to mind as they watched the assembly. They guessed some of the younger women had bought a dress two sizes too small and after getting in it, soaked it, so it would shrink some more. Stan and Marcy soon developed a code: when a woman walked by that was wearing such an outfit. One of them would imitate holding a pitcher and pouring it into a non-existent glass. I.e. the lady was poured into her clothes, filling every inch. They were a little surprised to see this kind of dress in church.

They couldn't see how anyone didn't die of heat stroke just sitting in church. The only fan was for the preacher, and it seemed as if none really cared if the windows were opened or not. Despite the 10 AM announced starting time, nothing happened until 10:30.

The benches were varnished wood. Someone had designed them so that they were horizontal on the bottom piece and vertical on the back. They were not designed for comfort, and not designed to sleep on. After about 10 minutes there would be a great uneasiness of sitting in such a position and a chance to stand to sing or greet one another was a welcome change. One could even invent such an excuse as going to the bathroom in order to get some relief for sitting very long. Now the bathroom was an outhouse down a very short path from the church. It was also visible by most of those sitting in the congregation. The condition and smell of that building does not warrant a report here. Suffice it to say, one really needed to use that little building and one did not linger long in the "little house."

Their late arrival was no concern to Frazer at all. It seems as if that was the normal thing. They had determined to sit as far in the back as they could, but the last two rows were already filled when they arrived. Frazer's family all sat together on a row about midway up the auditorium. They sat in the row behind them.

The song service was energetic with each song having about 15 verses that were evidently the same words. Song books were evidently privately owned, there were none in the pews for visitors to use. Actually having a song book wasn't necessary. If you didn't know the words, you just invented a sound and went along with everybody else.

The preacher got up and began a sermon with great enthusiasm.

Later as they reflected on the sermon, having a problem with the dialect, they decided that it wasn't on the issue of should ladies wear lipstick, but where lips stick. As it was, they were not sure the rest of the congregation heard the sermon at all.

The lady behind Stan and Marcy, screamed loudly, and stood up waving her arms. It about scared them out of their wits. Then she started wiggling and a jiggling in a way they had never seen before. When she got most of the way down the aisle she fell down and began to roll and moan on the ground. "Slain in the spirit" they called it, and Stan and Marcy had never seen anything like it in their Presbyterian upbringing. Then there were others, until the front of the church was filled with people and everywhere people were crying and carrying on.

The preacher was still preaching, but it was obvious nobody was paying attention. What little they caught of the sermon was a repetition of words that almost didn't make any sense. His heavy breathing and the cadence of his words were mesmerizing. They finally got their way through the service without joining those on the floor, and without having a heart attack or a heat stroke. Even though they were not dressed as warmly as the rest of the parishioners they were sweating profusely by the time the two hour service was over. They would have left sooner, but felt as guests they should stay until the end.

They had wanted to taste Vincy culture, and they felt they had a good taste of it by the time they had walked back to Frazer's house. Later they were to find that some of the more traditional churches were much more sedate - though the dress was still very formal, and very hot.

While the initial shock was something at the time, later they were to look back on it and think of it as something every tourist should do.

Funeral Service

While the exact timing of the funeral service that Stan and Marcy attended does not fit in this chronological order, it should be noted that funerals many times are not anticipated. They interrupt busy schedules, come at inopportune times, and sometimes mark some major changes for the living. For Stan and Marcy they had to put down their tools, and spend most of the day with the affairs of the funeral.

While they did attend church with the Frazer's, a funeral was not at all like what a regular service was about. For sure, it was unlike any service they had attended in the states. Frazer's father died and Stan and Marcy again put on the best that they had. By now Stan had gotten a suit sent from the states, and Marcy a formal dress. They dressed as best they could, but found that they were still not as classy as the Vincy's. Marcy was wondering where they got such outfits; she didn't see them in any of the stores she had stepped into.

The viewing of the body was held an hour before the scheduled time of the funeral. They went a half hour earlier than that, at Frazer's insistence. They found out later that was the only way to find a seat. The church would be packed an hour before the funeral. Any other church service, it would start late, not so with funerals. They always started on time.

When they came in the front door, there was a sign up book for all the viewers to sign. They duly registered their names and then entered the sanctuary. The coffin, with the deceased inside, was right there at the doorway. There was a crowd around the coffin and people were taking pictures. Stan and Marcy were asked by Frazer to stand by the coffin so he could take a picture of them with his deceased father. They obliged. They felt this a little macabre.

They sat down where they could feel a fan blowing, and were near an open window. They had learned some lessons about trying to keep cool. When the preacher entered the sanctuary the people stood, and the preacher led the processional down the aisle. Behind him were a couple of young men carrying a banner of some sort with the pallbearers moving the casket down the aisle.

The first song was to be sung standing, but it had hardly started, when the lady in front of them, who had appeared subdued, let out a blood curdling cry and sank back on the bench. She was sitting on the front edge of the seat, and leaned back, her head resting on the back of the pew. She had her head tilted back, was looking right at Stan. She let out another scream of grief. If Stan and Marcy had not gone to a previous church service this might have come as a total shock. Despite being in the middle of the row, he was ready to head for the exit. But extra pews had been brought in and pews were jammed together. There was no space to exit the row. The back entrance was jam packed with more people trying to get in, and Stan and Marcy would not be able to leave without creating even more of a traffic jam. They were stuck there for the rest of the funeral. This was scary stuff for them.

The lady covered her face with a large handkerchief, and continued to sob. Someone sat down next to her and tried to console her. Stan wasn't sure how the rest of the service was going to be conducted, as another lady up front also went into a swoon, followed by two others. But by the time the last verse was sung, everything was in order and the service continued. By now the casket was in the front of the building, and the pastor read some scripture as if nothing was happening around him.

No one seemed in a hurry, and specials were sung, some obviously not practiced, prior to the funeral. The pastor got up and delivered a sermon "A Safe Flight Home." The deceased was known to say those words whenever someone gave him a ride home and dropped him off near his home, on the side of a mountain. Stan knew where the man had lived, and it was like taking a small plane flight several hundred feet above the trees, only you would be in a car. You would be looking down at the top of trees, right beside the road. The pastor talked about

Reservation, Confirmation, Identification, and Embarkation. Simple enough that Stan remembered it for years. While sitting there he thought through his own mortal life and wondered about eternity. He knew that more than once he had almost left this world on "Final Flight."

When the sermon was over there was one last song. The casket was to be wheeled to the back of the church, but again, before the pastor had taken a few steps to the back of the sanctuary, the crying erupted again. This time there was even more crying and carrying on as the casket was rolled towards the doorway. The coffin was taken outside and put in the back of a hearse, and then began the processional to the grave site. They blocked the entire roadway, both coming and going traffic as they sang to the music coming out of the speakers on top of the hearse. It was very formal and solemn as they headed to the graveyard.

The congregation went to the grave site and there they gathered around the freshly dug grave. There were no "funeral plots." There had been reports of when they were digging the graves, finding bones and clothes of prior burials. There were no large markers giving date of birth, nor date of death. Sections of the cemetery were totally unmarked, but you could see where the land was uneven as each grave had a mound of dirt higher than the surroundings. Generations were buried on this sacred ground.

Some of the newer grave sites did have cement markers, and Stan and Marcy knew that Frazer would make sure his father had a proper marker put in place. But for most, there were no such markers. One could not come and find where a great grandfather was buried, unless they had somebody to point out the grave. Not one granite stone was in place, and not one bronze marker. Devoid of all markers were several generations, and all that could be said, was, a burial had taken place. Somewhere in the graveyard lay the bones of the dearly departed. All burials were registered at the Anglican Church, and which graveyard they were buried, but not the exact spot.

Again the preacher read some scripture and talked about eternity. There was a short prayer and the coffin was lowered into the ground, by whoever wanted to help. The grave diggers began shoveling the dirt on top of the coffin. The wailing began again, and continued until the last shovel of dirt was placed on top of the ground. There was a mound of earth on top of the ground that marked the spot where the deceased lay.

Without a PA system, someone began to lead singing and they sang several of the traditional hymns. Almost every burial had the same songs, almost totally irrespective of the particular religion a person was. Catholics, Methodists, Spiritual Baptists, Pentecostals had the same hymns when it came to burial.

There came a point when the lead singer ran out of songs to sing, and a drunk who, hadn't been at the service, took over the singing. He had come directly from a rum shop. He just took over the leading of the songs, complete with waving his hands. The crowd followed his lead.

When the task was finished and they had smoothed the mound of dirt as best they could, People began to file by and place flowers on the grave as they sang a song Stan and Marcy had never heard before. It was "Crown him with Roses." Again, they found this song to be sung at all funerals, again irrespective of the religion of the deceased. Then there were some candles placed in the ground and lit, and finally the congregation turned from the grave site and began the walk up the hill.

Stan and Marcy were up on the main road looking down over the grave site, and noticed that there was a rainbow that ended at the cemetery. Stan and Marcy were in a thoughtful mood that night. Stan would never forget the sermon "A Safe Flight Home."

Chapter Eight

Falling Tree Limbs

Stan and Marcy decided that they wanted to go to the beach for a day and just relax. Frazer was busy with the marina, but his wife was glad for the opportunity because the children were in school, and would not be able to come. They decided to go in the middle of the week and hoped to have the beach to themselves.

Stan had a hammock that rolled into a very small ball when not in use. It was convenient to take with them. A couple of good books, a change of clothes and towels, and they were almost set. They stopped at Kentucky Fried Chicken to buy lunch. It was simple, go out for the most part of the day, and eat lunch in a place that the people back home would pay thousands of dollars to trade places with them. They did forget to take the camera.

Mrs. Frazer was a chatty person, and Marcy liked the female companionship. Stan was in the back seat of the vehicle already tuned out. He had his CD player with fresh batteries and some CDs to listen to. His brother, Ken, had just sent him some <u>Popular Mechanics</u> and a new <u>Multihulls</u> magazine with the Sunday funnies. Life couldn't get any better than this. This was a day off, with no obligations, and they were going to enjoy the bright sunshine and the beautiful beach.

Mt. Wynne is on the opposite side of the island, and the roads were not exactly the greatest. Some places if you met an oncoming car you had to back up to where the road was wide enough to pass safely, and backing up was not exactly the easiest thing to do. The roads were not marked; there were no warning signs, no curb markings, and no center lines. One side would be a rocky cliff wall and the other would be about 300 feet straight into the deep blue Caribbean Sea. Stan's driveway back in the states was wider. When he wasn't listening to the music, or reading he couldn't believe what he was seeing – and couldn't believe that this was actually the major road on the leeward side of the island.

Mrs. Frazer didn't seem to notice any of the dangers. Everything was as it has always been for her, while this was a different experience for Stan and Marcy.

Surprising to Stan and Marcy was the hour drive to Mt. Wynne. Even though there were no speed limits, the sharp curves going up and coming down mountain roads kept them from going very fast in the car. They even met cows on the road, and sometimes sheep tied to a tree beside the road. The sheep would stretch to the other side for the green grass, their tether rope blocking the road.

They arrived at Mt. Wynne beach and Mrs. Frazer was delighted to see that tourism people had put in some benches since her last trip to the beach. The Department of Tourism was really trying to upgrade the tourist sites.

There were some new benches put up under the trees, but some were occupied by workers. Their tools were scattered around, and they were eating lunch. The workers immediately indicated they could park there and sit. This would have been their first choice to park, but they didn't want to ask the workers to move, so Mrs. Frazer chose to park near the water without any benches. There were no tables, so the trunk was their table and with a couple of folding chairs, they were in business.

After eating Stan tied his hammock between two trees. He was shaded, had an off shore wind blowing to keep him cool, no sign of rain and things were looking good. He lay out in the hammock and got himself comfortable. Marcy got in the car on the passenger side and leaned her seat as far back as it would go and was definitely going for a nap.

Mrs. Frazer had a good book. She had a thermos with coffee, which was unusual for a Vincy to drink coffee this time of day. With some Crix crackers she was enjoying her time out.

Stan noticed that the workers had moved off the benches, and were back at work. Without power tools, they were using cutlasses to trim bushes, so the park area remained quiet. There was a couple down further on the beach, with a couple of small children. Other than that, they had the beach to themselves. No phone to ring, no beggars to come by, nobody stopping and asking for a drink of water, or begging for food.

Eventually the workers moved out of sight and sound, the couple left with the children and they were left alone with the wind in the trees, and waves lapping at the beach, and the temperature was very comfortable. Their drinks were still cold, with ice to spare; they had eaten and were satisfied. Stan was sure that a millionaire could not be enjoying the day anymore than they were. This was totally relaxing.

This is what it was suppose to be like in the tropics. Lounging under a shade tree, not a care in the world, and he decided to start with reading the funny papers. He decided that this was great that his brother had sent them, and was going to remember to ask him to continue to send them in the future. Only thing he was missing was someone with a camera to take his picture so he could send it back home to his friends. This surely was a picture post card moment, with the words in his mind "wish you were here." Actually his thoughts were, glad you're not here, and this is total peace and quiet.

Stan busied himself with reading the Sunday funnies. They were several weeks' old, but new jokes to him. His brother had really picked up on a good thing to send him. While perusing through his newspaper, he had this thought. Not a voice, not like someone coming up to him and talking to him, but a very clear thought. "Your life could change in an instant if a tree limb broke". Since that was not in his reading material he stopped reading and looked up above his head, and noticed a scarcity of limbs, and they were very high. Maybe only one limb could be of any danger to him.

Since the thought did not seem to carry any urgency to move, or getting out of the hammock, he kept his comfortable position, and continued reading.

After a while he stopped reading again and looked up into the expanse above. The trees were swaying in the gentle breeze, and then there was a loud crack. He watched a branch, a good 30' up, break off and fall. It was at least eight feet long and more. The major bulk of the branch was as big as a 3"x3" and considering the distance falling, could do some real damage. He watched it hit the ground right between the two benches the workers had been sitting, right where their first choice had been to park. It hit with such force it dug a hole in the ground and bounced.

He knew immediately that by being in his present location, he had avoided serious injury or possible death. There was no way he could have avoided the falling tree limb if they had parked over by the benches and he had strung his hammock in the logical place, between the two benches.

The noise woke his wife who sat up in the car. Mrs. Frazer came out of her chair with an exclamation, "what was that?" Marcy came out of the car to look. They all decided that if they had taken the kind offer of the workers and used the benches, Stan would probably be underneath that huge limb.

Yes, death stalks us all, and Stan realized he had eluded death one more time. At the least, "Your life could change in an instant if a tree limb broke."

When he picked up his things to go, they took serious note of the fallen branch, and knew except for choosing the second location; Stan would have been seriously hurt, or worse.

Admiralty Bay

Pizza

One day when Stan took a short break from fiber glassing in a bunk, Frazer came. They, as many times before, compared growing up and their different lifestyles. Stan mentioned that he really liked Pizza and had missed it there in SVG. He had tried the place right across from the airport, and there was one that went out of business just after he arrived that was downtown, but he felt like they just fell short of his expectations. *Pizza Hut* hadn't yet discovered St. Vincent, and *Dominoes, Papa's Pizza* and *Little Ceasar's* and the other franchises were unheard of.

"Let's go get a pizza for lunch." Frazer suggested.

Stan without thinking said, "Where?" He was sure he had found all the pizza places.

"We need to leave at 11 and get there before the crowd." He really hadn't answered Stan's question, but he had deflected enough that Stan was intrigued.

"I need to call my wife and she could go with us."

"No," Frazer replied, "this is a guy thing, and for now you can keep it a secret."

Stan kept track of his time, and had his tools put away, and had dressed for the van ride into town; No work clothing, no itchy fiberglass shirts, he had to look and smell presentable.

Frazer came by, and the two walked out to the road and almost immediately caught a van into town. It was the usual ride, and the van was full, the music was loud, and people were crammed together. They only made a couple short stops. Only once did Stan and Frazer have to step out of the van so passengers could get off and others get on. They got off by the Ju-C plant in town, before the regular bus stop. A short walk to the Grenadines wharf and Stan and Frazer walked directly on the *Admiral* ferry. Stan was now intrigued.

"Where are we going?" Stan asked.

"To Bequia."

"That is where the Pizza place is?"

"*Mac's Pizzeria*, Considered to be the best Pizza in the country."

"Cool."

The two had a great time swapping jokes and telling stories during the hour crossing that went quickly. Bequia had a mountain that came right down to the sea, and the *Admiral* passed within seventy five yards. It was the rainy season, and it was green veranda that came right down the side of mountain, ending where the rocks began. There were places on the outcroppings where vegetation grew and birds had made nests. St. Vincent was easily visible behind them. It was quite a sight to Stan. They came up to a navigational marker, and they turned left and headed into the lower part of the bay. Over to the right was Lower Bay, a mile long white sandy beach. They were headed up to the middle of Admiralty Bay, where the pier awaited. On both sides were hundreds of yachts anchored. Stan was awed. Majestic hills or mountains, depending on your upbringing, covered with green vegetation, and this sandy beach on the right, and surrounded by yachts. This indeed was paradise. The *Admiral* moved up top of the closed off bay, and very skillfully docked at the pier.

Frazer had brought out his cell phone back at the navigational marker and called Mac's. He placed an order for the pizza; pepperoni on one half, ground beef on the other, with a double layer of cheese.

They departed the boat and walked along a short, sandy beach, with trees overhanging the sand. There was a small road, and a walkway, alongside the beach. Here vans were not the usual means of public conveyance. Transport here were trucks with built in seats in the back and a roof overhead, much like what Stan drove, but in much better condition. There were tie down curtains when it rained, for the sides. The drivers were courteous, and had small stools to help with getting up in the back of the truck. They all parked next to the dock, up under the trees. Taxi drivers would call out to them as they walked by, "Would you like transport?"

Many of the drivers recognized Frazer, and gave a greeting.

When they ran out of beach, there was a walkway that led to shops further up the waterfront. There were curio shops, and tourist traps, and outdoor restaurants, all gaily painted in pastel colors. The water lapped gently at their feet. At high tide, and high winds the sidewalk would be submerged in the water. However, here and there were small docks with dinghies tied to them, the owners gone ashore, waiting for the return trip to one of the yachts out at anchor. Friendly people passed them on the walk way, others sitting out in the open air restaurants would greet them as they walked by.

They shortly arrived at *Mac's Pizzeria* and found their pizza ready.

While sitting there, looking over the bay, filled with boats, Stan was entranced at all that he saw. He told Frazer, "I can't wait to bring Marcy here."

Frazer agreed, "This a great place. It has been here awhile. Yachts call in on their radios and order pizza. The dinghy dock's make it easy to come in to pick it up, or eat right here. Others use cell phones. Some just drop by. But the pizza itself is the attraction, and by now you would have to agree."

Stan would agree.

The ferry had docked at 12:30; they had about an hour and a half to the two o'clock ferry. They would be back in St. Vincent by three and could be back at the boat for an hour's worth of work if Stan so desired.

Then Frazer had this idea. "Don't tell Marcy."

"Why not?"

"Keep this as a secret, something you have done, that she will never have to know about."

"We have no secrets. We share everything."

Frazer then came up with the great idea. "Aren't you going to write a book someday about all this, and what it is like here?"

"Yes."

"Well, don't let her read the rough drafts, or proof read it. Put this story in the book, and one day when she picks it up she will read of the pizza trip to *Mac's* and THEN she will know.

Stan liked the idea and made note of it. One day he would write a book, and his wife would only discover this little secret when she read it!

Admiralty Bay up Close

Robbery

Stan always made sure his tools were locked away if he wasn't right there. If someone else was around the boat yard, all tools were out of sight except for the one in his hand. He didn't want to be the victim of the "five finger discount."

As far as St. Vincent was concerned robbery wasn't a big problem, but Stan and Marcy noticed almost all windows, and most doorways had steel rebar to keep out intruders. When in town, they were careful, but noted that pick pockets, and purse snatchers, were almost unheard of.

However, one particular night there was a man outside the bathroom window. Stan actually saw the man and knew he was out of place, because they were up almost two full floors from the ground. Stan met him at the window, when he tried to crawl in. It was the only window in the house without re-bar. Maybe Frazer had thought nobody could get to the window. But there were two thieves. A short man was standing on the shoulders of the tall one, and he was standing on a 55 gallon drum they had taken off the back of the truck that Stan had thrown garbage into. They had placed a board across the top of the drum and the tall man was standing on that. There was an altercation, but be it said, the man didn't make it into the window. The man trying to come in was small, and was no match for Stan. Stan thought he might be a teen-ager, but later found him to be in his mid 50s.

When the thieves were discovered, the tall one underneath ran away leaving the short guy hanging from the window. Stan hit him in the ribs a few times with a hammer. Then the man let go and somehow missed the drum, but landed on his side on the rocky lawn. The taller man was long gone. The little guy got up and launched a rock against the window, but it hit the metal parts of the window and glanced away. During this time there was almost no noise made. The struggle was in almost complete silence. It didn't wake the Frazers. Stan's wife knew what was going on, and had curled up at the head of the bed where she could not be seen and could not see the scuffle.

The following Tuesday, Stan was sick in bed all day. He just wasn't feeling good and slept most of the time. There was some kind of function going on at one of the children's school and the family was going, and Marcy wanted to go, so Stan said to go ahead he was ok to stay by himself.

He was making some popcorn as they were leaving the driveway. He had it in a metal container when he sat down to watch TV. He was sure he was safe, it was barely 7:00PM and even though it was just barely dark, it was still early. He didn't think in terms of safety, and that those robbers would return. The only thing not locked and closed was the sliding door that the Frazer's family and Marcy had just left open as they left. The porch light was on, and the living room light was on. He was sitting in the living room and surely no one would try to rob with a person present. It seemed as if he had no more than sat down, than a man stepped into the living room with a 2x2 above his head screaming!

His first thought was "older brother" of the man in the window from just last Saturday. He immediately rushed the man, using the metal container to block any blow the man with the 2x2 would attempt. Surprised, the man was still in the doorway with the stick above his head, when Stan's charge slammed him against the railing on the porch. By now, Stan had dropped the metal pan, and had the man's arms where he wanted them. With a background in wrestling, and some serious training in the military, he knew the next move was to step across his body and body slam him to the ground and break his arm in one move. He never got the chance.

The little man in the window from last Saturday suddenly appeared with a gun in hand!

"I'm going to shoot you." He said. Stan believed he would, or at least hold the gun on him, and the other man beat him to death, so he ran. Evidently the guy with the 2x2 hit him a glancing blow on the head as he headed into the kitchen.

Things got into a kind of blur; he ran through the kitchen and tried to get out the back door. However, there were three locks on the door, and he just couldn't get them opened in time.

The man with the gun had run through the kitchen, still yelling "I'm going to shoot you." Stan finally gave up and turned and faced the two men. Neither was wearing masks, and that concerned him a great deal. If they weren't afraid to show their faces, maybe they didn't intend to leave a witness behind.

"What do you want?" Stan asked them.

"Where is the money?" The little guy with the gun asked.

Now Stan knew the man was serious, he was looking down the barrel of the revolver, and he could see the bullets in the cylinder. But he had to work hard not to laugh.

He thought: "That was a good question! Where is the money? Maybe I could help you look for it!"

And just someday he would want to ask someone in authority "Where is the money?" Because he knew he didn't have any.

They wanted money, but he had none on himself. He led them into the bedroom and got his wallet. About $35 E.C. was all that was in it. They took Marcy's purse that she had left behind and fumbled through it. They took out a business envelop and laid it on the top of the dresser, with some other items. They never looked into the envelope and never noticed it was filled with E.C. folding money!

They went through the shelves in the room, where they had folded and stacked their clothes. They were open shelves, not even a curtain to shield from prying eyes. They were just little cubicles going up beside the "closet". It too, was just an open closet without a door. This simple closet was a simple addition Stan had put in the room before Marcy arrived.

They had again found no money.

When Marcy came home, and she entered the bedroom she asked, "Did they have a seeing eye dogs with them? They must be blind. Look from here, across the room, I can see U.S. money sticking out from underneath some underwear." They had looked right through that stack of clothes!!

The thieves spent some time going through the rest of the house. They took his watch, and then handed it back. It did look cheap, and all the extra hands for minutes, stopwatch functions, and dates had ceased to work some time ago. It wasn't even one of the newer digital watches; it had two hands that worked. It told hour and minutes of the hour, and that was all.

They took his Coast Guard ring, and his wedding band. After some time, he called the tall man back in the room and asked for his rings back. The man reached into his mid-calf black, rubber boots and pulled out a plastic bag. He noticed the weight of the Coast Guard ring and kept it. However, he handed back the wedding ring.

Having been sick all day, Stan was just not feeling well, which probably protected him so he could continue living on the island. If he had killed one or both, they probably had friends and would come looking for him. When they took him into Frazer's bedroom, he knew where Frazer kept his cutlass at all times. The man with the gun turned his back on him when they left the bedroom; Stan could have easily given him a chop, and then taken the gun and gone after robber number two. But, instead he just followed him out of the room.

The other robber was looking through the kitchen cabinets and found a stack of CDs and asked Stan to get him a bag. Stan opened the kitchen closet to get a plastic bag for the man. The robber was on his knees looking through the cabinet. The man paid him no mind, and didn't look at what Stan was doing. Stan opened the closet in the kitchen and noticed a hatchet hanging inside. He knew that one well placed blow and the man would be severely injured or dead. He was still on his knees, head down looking in the small cupboard, and not watching Stan at all. Stan didn't know where in the house the guy with the gun was located, but again, he just didn't feel like doing anything.

Whatever he was sick with, he was still not feeling well. He let the opportunity slip away.

They really didn't get much. Later at the trial, it would be easy to figure that if they had regular jobs they would have made a lot more per hour working, than what they gained by stealing. Since most of the items stolen were recovered, they only got to enjoy the money they found. Stan got back his Coast Guard Ring. It had his name inside it.

Stan knew that death was there in the house that night, but in the end it was cheated by all three. The thieves took some material things, but Stan was relieved they didn't take his life.

As a theologian said: "Today I was robbed."
"I am thankful that while he took all I had, it wasn't much."
"I am thankful He took my money and not my life."
"I am thankful it was he who robbed, and not I."

Dogs

The next day Stan went up the road that the robbers took when they left. Not knowing the area he stayed on the "main" road, not taking the goat trail over the hill. The "main road" he discovered was a private drive. He could see where it ended at a house, where evidently some neighbors lived. He had seen them drive by a couple of times.

He slanted off towards the goat trail and was out in the grass when he noticed the dogs barking. Three dogs were barking and running right at him. He was inclined to run, but figured the dogs would outrun him and in fleeing, the dogs would even be more inclined to nip at his heels, or run him down, and all three pounce on him. He stood his ground and waited. They did not sound friendly at all. His heart began to race; He did his best to remain calm. Two of the dogs he recognized as roaming free in the neighborhood, and had been around him at other times. The third dog was the unknown. When they came up to him he acted friendly but they did not. They were directly in front of him, which helped. They did not surround him. He extended his hand in a friendly gesture, but remembering what he had read, he kept his fingers in a fist. A dog could really rake his fingers over good if they decided to bite. But a fist is a little harder to get in the mouth. He also knew if a dog bit, he would jam the fist down its throat and break his lower jaw if he could. That still left the other two to do him serious harm. He knew he was in a tight predicament.

The dogs stared at him and kept barking, not very peaceable looking at all. One of the two "friendliest" was at his right hand and the other on the left. The third dog never approached close enough to lick his hand, and continued barking and growling. He was just far enough away that one good jump would put him at Stan's throat. And he acted like that is exactly what he wanted to do.

The two that knew him began to lick his hands, one on the left and the other on the right. The third dog continued to bark and growl, like he was encouraging the two to attack, but they did not. But the two dogs were not exactly given to a peaceable gesture either. They would lick his hand and move back just a little bit, and sit and growl. Spit was coming out the sides of their mouths. All three were definitely showing a splendid array of teeth. Then they would move the few inches back to his hand and lick it again, and then move back a few inches and sit and growl some more, and more spit dripped to the ground.

Stan was beginning to wonder how this was going to end. He could not see how he was just going to walk away from this. The dogs showed no signs of going away. The two kept licking his hand and then moving a few inches away, and growl very menacingly and then coming close and licking his hand again. Stan was not nervous, and tried to show that he really wasn't scared. He knew with three against one, this could turn ugly in a very short order. The two "friendliest" were not his concern. It was the third dog, directly in front of him that concerned him. He kept his distance. He was sitting, and spit was coming out the side of his mouth as he growled. He did not come up and lick Stan's hand one time.

In the midst of all this, he was aware how hot the sun had gotten as he was standing in the open field. The sweat was trickling down his back and he couldn't tell if it was nerves or if it was just the sun.

When Stan had given up any hope of walking away unharmed, the owner called their dogs. Immediately one turned and went, the other two stayed for just a short while, and with a final growl, they also retreated. The dog right in front of him was the last to leave. Stan was very glad to see them go. He figured out how to return to the house without going near where the dogs lived. Since being bit once while on a bicycle, Stan was never a fan of dogs, and never really liked dogs. He knew he had escaped serious injury or even death from this incident. It was something that would be forever engraved on his mind, standing in an open field with two dogs alternating between licking his hand, and growling at him like they would love to jump for his throat. The third dog was the most unknown, and all of his intentions seemed to be to inflict bodily harm. He was so thankful to be able to turn and walk away. His hands were wet and dripping from saliva of the two dogs. He was glad that death was unsuccessful once again.

Car Wreck

Frazier took them from time to time in his car to various places. Stan and Marcy were always amazed at the speed at which the vehicles traveled, and how narrow the roads were. Yet there were few fatalities on the island. Driving on the left side took some getting used to. It seemed at every turn Frazier went to the wrong side, and even though they trusted his driving, they cringed inside, expecting to meet someone head on.

They noticed the absence of center lines and shoulder markings. None. When you got to a work site, there may or may not be a workman to motion you on, or to stop. If there were a "flagman" he had no reflective vest, no flag in hand, and you were not sure if he was just a spectator waving you on, or part of the repair crew. There were no flags, or cones. Sometimes you might notice a red rag tied to a tree beside the road. Many times you just met the construction.

Once there was a large water pipe dug up in the middle of the road. The ditch was over 6' deep, and when the end of the working day came, the workers went home, leaving the hole. There was a mound of dirt on one side of the hole, effectively making it a one way road. At one end there was a mound of dirt, but at the other end, the chasm was open for any unsuspecting car. There wasn't a single flag, cone, or light to mark this danger spot, at either end. One direction you could drive into a six foot hole. In the other direction you could hit a six foot pile of dirt in the road in your lane. It was several days before they got the pipe fixed, and it seems as if the driver's knew of the ditch in the middle of the road, and the pile of dirt and avoided it. There were no reported accidents during this period of time.

Most sides of the roadways had deep ditches for water drainage. There were no grates on the top, just open drains. Truck tires would not reach to the bottom of the ditch, and more than once a vehicle would be hung up on the frame with a wheel dangling over the ditch. While they thought of the drains as deep, when a real downpour occurred, they would fill all the way to the top, and in many places overflow. Deep open drains didn't leave many options when meeting oncoming vehicles. Some places were next to a cliff, with a 300' drop down the side. The other side was deep drainage ditch with no cover. You had to thread the needle very carefully.

One day while going to town they met an oncoming car in their lane, speeding. It came around a blind corner, and

BLAM, the accident happened. None were injured, but almost immediately Frazier and the other driver got into a shouting match. They stood toe to toe and hurled words at each other.

The police were called and since there was no police vehicle at that station, they found a convenient van headed in the direction they needed to go, flagged it down and finally arrived on scene. Even if there had been a police vehicle, there would have to be a licensed driver at the station willing to risk driving the government vehicle. The driver had to pay for it if it was involved in an accident. Police resorted to taking vans when necessary. Neither vehicle had moved after they had stopped. They were to leave the vehicles alone until a policeman painted where the tires were on the pavement, while traffic was flagged around the vehicles. The police marked the position of the four tires of each car and listened to the two drivers argue. He informed them they had 48 hours to produce proof of insurance, and 3 days to produce their driver's license at any police station on the island.

All of the debris was on Frazier's side of the road, which would be a good indication of whose fault it was.

They were told to report to the station the next day.

They had to bend the fender away from the front tires so they could drive the car. They were thankful the radiator was not punctured. The side mirror was ripped away, and major damage was done to the driver's door.

The next day upon arrival, all of them gave a statement as to their version of the accident. First Frazer and then Stan gave their story, individually, in a room with just the witness and the police. The police carefully hand wrote it out, and when they were satisfied with it, they signed their individual statements. The driver of the other car was then called into the room and gave his version, and signed his.

They went to the accident site, and measurements were made from the point of impact, to where the vehicles were stopped. Each point was measured also in relationship to the width of the road. All drivers and witnesses confirmed the measurements as true. All this was carried out as vans, trucks and cars passed by, and not one flag or cone was used to warn drivers to slow down.

Then because they were in Frazier's home, they heard the rest of the story. No tickets were issued by the police. He would have to get a lawyer and sue the other owner in court in order to collect his money. The docket remained full, so it would be three to six months before the court case was heard, or longer. Then because you got a judgment in your favor didn't mean that you could collect the money.

Then there was the problem of repair. There were some good auto body shops on the island, and in this case they all said that what they needed was a driver's side door. When it comes to car parts, the owner was responsible for finding his own parts. Frazer had trouble finding a door for his particular model. The end result was that for the next few months the driver had to crawl out the passengers' side of the car which was not very convenient at all. In the end, the car was fixed and life went on as though this was perfectly normal.

This was a typical case of "you fix yours, and I'll fix mine."

Elfie

Dog Fight

Mrs. Frazer had a dog that she walked every day. While they were staying at the Frazer's, from time to time, Marcy would walk the dog, Elfie. Stan just didn't want to lead a dog on a daily walk.

One evening, just after she had left the house, Stan heard some screaming outside. At first he thought it was just another man beating a woman which was not all that uncommon in St. Vincent. So he just sat there watching some more TV. However, as the screaming reached a crescendo, he realized that his wife was walking the dog, and that it was probably his wife's voice he was hearing. He had never heard her yell like that.

He jumped up, and ran out the door.

Not really clear in all the details later, he did remember enough of the scene all too well. Elfie was upside down underneath a larger dog. The larger dog had Elfie's throat in a death grip with his teeth and was not turning loose. The remains of an umbrella were on the ground that Marcy had used to beat on the strange dog. There were a couple of Vincies standing around that were doing nothing. His wife still had Elfie's walking chain in her hand, and was just standing there screaming "No!"

Stan does not recall just how it happened after that, but the next thing he knew he had the larger dog by the throat in his left hand and was beating it in the head with his right. He had straddled the dog and as Stan awoke to what was happening, he realized that this was a large dog. In fact, very large, and it was lying sideways on the ground. This was a full grown, well fed, Doberman Pincher. As he straddled the dog he was aware that his knees almost did not touch the ground. He continued to hit and hit on the dog until he thought it was dead. Then it rolled over just a little. He hit it some more. He also realized that if he let this dog up, it was not headed for Elfie, it would come after him. He asked his wife to hand him a big stone so he could kill it, but she would not.

After awhile he had hit the dog enough he was having trouble hanging on, and was getting tired.

The owner had heard the screaming and checked out the window of their house, and discovered that their Doberman had gotten out of his cow chain. They heard a foreigner screaming and somehow connected the two events. The son now showed up on scene, taking his time walking down the hill.

Stan stood up and let the dog go. The dog amazingly stood up and staggered away. It acted like it was drunk. It went awhile before it went off into an open field and sat down. The owner then dragged the dog home. For the next three days the dog barked with a raspy voice. It wouldn't eat. It stood out in the rain and wouldn't go in his dog house. The neighborhood talked about it for years afterwards.

Eventually, the dog recovered.

Stan let the incident fade into the background, as he realized that he had fought a Doberman Pincher with his bare hands, and had walked away alive from the incident without a scratch. While there was much Vincy criticism of the event, Stan just told which dog it was and invited the critic to go and take on the dog even while chained up - with their bare hands. It was something to recount back in the states over a cup of coffee.

Death by a Doberman pincher didn't seem a possibility until he read in the papers that someone had jumped over a fence, evidently with the intent to rob. He couldn't get back over the fence in time to avoid the Doberman that came at him. They found his body the next day. The news, complete with pictures, was in the paper by the end of the week. Stan now counts himself as a very fortunate man who avoided death once again, in this foreign land.

Chapter Nine

Worms - Southern Grenadines – Exploding Battery

When the first month had gone by, Stan and his wife had put in some long hours. From almost first light to dark they had worked. They had even rigged lights at night, but too many bugs were attracted to the light to do any fiberglass work. The bugs stuck to the wet fiberglass before it dried, and the next morning they would have to sand them all out.

Stan had run long distance in high school and learned to just keep pushing. He could ignore the pain and keep working. Generally by the next morning after a good night's rest, he was ready to work again. But the constant pressure to get done by the end of the month, to be able to sail north before the hurricane season came, kept Stan working at a steady grinding rate. When the month had come and gone, and it seemed as if they weren't half way done the pressure began to mount.

One day when Stan had finished for the day and drove home feeling really tired. He felt that it would be easier to just roll out of the truck than to try to stand up. Despite the truck being a medium height off the ground, when he parked it next to a small wall, the wall was easier to reach than the footrest on the truck. And it seemed easier to just roll out of the truck and that is exactly what he did. He rolled out of the truck onto all fours. Then using the door for support he pulled himself up to standing height. The pain permeated his body, and he just stood there for awhile. He was on the verge of tears he hurt so badly. It was worse than any cross country race he remembered. He almost crawled into the house, but decided against it.

When he came inside Frazer had some company, and Mrs. Frazer was putting together some food, and was asking him what he wanted to eat for supper. He really didn't want to talk to anyone. He just wanted to go and lie down and see if sleep would take the aching pain away. Mr. Frazer introduced him to the company, but to this day Stan cannot remember their names. He begged a late supper, as he wanted to take a long shower, but mostly he wanted to rest. It was after this experience that he and Marcy decided that just maybe they could tune back the work load.

Work was progressing at a good rate, but they realized that they just were not going to get it done so soon. And they decided that the pressure of trying to get it done by a certain date was their own built in pressure. Being a work-a-holic was what they had done in the states, and what they wanted to do here was to enjoy St. Vincent. They began to keep less hours working hard at the job. They even sometimes quit work in the afternoon when the sun was hot, and came back a few hours in the late afternoon when the sun wasn't so brutal.

Stan began to notice that he just didn't feel like working some days. He felt like he had a low grade fever, and finally a visit to the doctor was in order. Other than feeling like he had been drug through a knot hole, he couldn't describe his condition to the doctor. Even while going to the doctor, he didn't feel like getting up and doing anything that day.

The basic medical system was a socialist health care system, but, on the advice of Frazer, he avoided the health clinic right up the street. He found out later that the people at the free health clinic, in order to see the doctor when he came one time a week on Thursday, arrived as early as 5am to get in line. To arrive later than 6am was to be so far back in line, that maybe you wouldn't see the doctor that day. You would have to wait until the following week. The doctor came around 9am. Sometimes he didn't come at all. Stan wondered what did you do if you were really sick, and it wasn't Thursday? He noticed that the people sat or stood outside the clinic. There were no chairs and they either sat on the ground, or sat on the curbing. There was very little room inside for a few patients. The smelly restrooms were hidden at the back of the clinic. There was no TV to watch, no magazines, and later in the day, no shade from the sun while standing and waiting.

There were private doctors and Frazer recommended one.

He went to the house where Frazer said the doctor lived. The house was a on a narrow two-lane street that was busy and there was no place to park. Stan had to park some distance away and walk up to the house. There was a sign hanging in the doorway to the garage with the hours the doctor was in and an arrow pointing down the steps to the basement area.

The doctor ran his office out of the basement of his house. There was a small area where waiting patients could sit and watch TV or read. There was no secretary to give him any forms. None. No forms to fill out, no questions about insurance, and it was obvious it was a cash deal. No credit cards were used here. Somehow the people waiting knew who was before them, and when you came, you could figure out where on the waiting list you were. Hours were 7am - 12 noon, and from 3pm – 7pm, Monday through Saturday. Only one doctor, there was no nurses and no secretary. The doctor filled out a 4x6 card with your name, date, and recommended treatment. That was the total paper work.

He paid the doctor directly, as there wasn't a secretary. The doctor even had to get out his wallet and make change for the money that Stan gave him. If Stan needed a receipt, the doctor would have given him one.

The private doctor sent him to give some blood at a lab, and told him they would wait and see what the report said. The doctor did report that the flu was going around, and he just might be a borderline case. Stan was amazed the doctor only charged $60 E.C. which is about $25 U.S. for the visit.

He went to the lab and found it almost cold with air conditioning, very unusual. He waited in a short line and paid $100 E.C., or about $38 U.S. He was told to come and collect his results in three days.

So Stan returned to work for the rest of the day. It was a kind of mind-over-matter type of work. He could have just as easily laid the sander down, and lay next to it and gone to sleep. The next couple of days were about the same. No change of diet, or drink, or routine got him out of this tired feeling.

After the three days were up, he went to collect his results at the lab. Much to his surprise they gave him the reports in an unsealed envelope. The numbers didn't mean much, but they looked like they were all within the normal range. He asked what he had to do with the report. The lab secretary stated the fact as if he should have known already. "Take them to your doctor."

The next day he was back at the doctor's office, earlier in the day so he wouldn't have to wait so long. The doctor did keep long hours, with a 7am opening time. When Stan went in the doctor weighed him, something he didn't do the first time. The doctor took his blood pressure, and looked at the results of the lab report.

He then cleared his throat and said, "You have no infections in your body that we can tell. Are you still feeling tired?"

"Yes, I have to drag myself out of bed, and I just can't work like I use to."

"I don't want to insult you, or make you feel bad; because there are many ways you could have contracted what I think you have, worms."

Stan was a little surprised about the doctor's diagnosis.

"Worms." He repeated.

"You could have gotten the worms from the water, from getting your hands dirty, walking barefoot, or not washing fresh fruit or vegetables before eating them." The doctor continued, "Yes, worms, and you need to take Zentel. You can buy them at any pharmacy, they are cheap, and they won't hurt you."

Stan left wondering how the doctor could come to such a conclusion, but decided to try his advice. He went to the pharmacy store and bought a box with the prescribed dosage and took them with a glass of water. When he got home, he went to bed because he was feeling tired. When he woke up, he was feeling great and was ready to go to work. To say he was amazed would be an understatement.

Barrouallie

Southern Grenadines

Stan and Marcy decided on one of their days off, to take a trip to go explore the Southern Grenadines. It had been highly recommended and the trip was simple enough. They would fly down to Union Island, and Captain Yannis would have someone meet them at the airport then they would be taken to the 60" catamaran, and be given a breakfast brunch. It turned out to be a great trip. The waves and wind were just right and the trip to the first stop, Mayreau, was without incident, but with spray once in a while climbing over the bow was exhilarating. They were thinking, "This is what tourists pay thousands of dollars to see and feel." The first stop was a small island of about 300 people. For the most part they snorkeled, but not much in the way of fish, as the bottom was all sandy. The anchorage was excellent, and the Catamaran pulled right up to the beach. One point of the island, they could see across a narrow spit of land, and see the waves pounding on the windward side. They thought of this as a place to return to with *Susan* when they were ready. If you didn't own a boat, and wanted to see big fish, this was the way to do it.

The trip then went to Tobago Keys. The boat again pulled up to the beach and they walked down to the sand on the ladder built into the front of the catamaran. They walked across a sandy island with scrub tress full of iguanas. Here the snorkeling was the best they had ever seen. Several years it had been voted the best dive area to visit in the Caribbean. Fishing was not allowed. To have a spear gun anywhere near here was to invite a severe fine. Line fishing was also not to be done. They had never before seen so many large fish, in such large schools. Lunch was served aboard the Cat before departure for Palm Island.

Palm Island was for the rich and famous. They could get off the boat and walk the beach, but were not allowed above the high tide mark. People stayed in individual cottages and without phone or interruptions. If they wanted something they put up a flag, and a steward would come and get what they wanted. If there was a phone call for them, a flag would also be hoisted, and then the tourist could come at his leisure and accept the call, or call back. It was managed by John Caldwell. John became known for his book "Desperate Voyage." It is about his experiences of intending to sail solo from Panama to Australia on his first sailboat trip. It seemed to be the only way he could find a passage to get to Australia to his wife. On this voyage he encountered a hurricane and lost his mast and much of his food. Sad to say, he didn't make it to Australia in the boat because he had no control over the boat when it went aground and was shipwrecked. But, he did find some transportation to Australia. Later he and his wife were on a voyage around the world (in a different boat) and ended up in the West Indies. After several years of chartering their boat, they talked the Vincy government into letting him have sole use of the island to change it from swamps and mosquitoes to a luxury resort, which they did.

Then from Palm Island, there was a short trip back to Union Island, and then an evening meal on board before a short ride to the airport. It was breath-taking to watch the Grenadine Islands from the air, and Stan and Marcy drank in their beauty.

As they neared St. Vincent, Stan thought they were almost going to land on the water. One end of the runway was almost at the water's edge. The pilot gave it more throttle to keep it in the air. That meant the landing speed was now a little high, and then the cross wind gust hit them. The plane hit and bounced sideways. The pilot over corrected and added more power to get airborne. He tried to steady the plane. When the wheels touched the second time Stan was going to learn firsthand what it means to have a life that would have a lot of "what if's" in it.

The plane blew a tire and almost took a ninety degree turn towards the grass. The pilot immediately throttled back on the power and started cutting switches off. The plane's wheels were off the runway! The plane hit some very soggy ground from all the torrential rains the island had been receiving, and the tire dug into the ground and snapped the landing gear. The pilot got the electrical switches killed before the plane began plowing up the grass. When the front wheel contacted the ground, it too buried into the soft ground and broke. Somehow the plane did not flip over, but for a while it was held up at an angle that approached a head over heels landing. The loose luggage slid to the front of the plane. In the confines of the plane, people were screaming. Stan knew that with the landing speed at over 100 mph, things were happening very fast. Somehow the plane spun around and finally stopped. It was heading in the same direction as it had come; only it was now out in the grassy area.

People were screaming and yelling and trying to get out the doors. Stan and Marcy were near a window under the wing. They waited their turn to get out at an emergency exit. The plane was lying partly on one side, making exiting the door an easy step to the ground. The wing tip was bent a little and was resting on the ground.

The fire truck from the airport took almost five minutes to get there. By then almost everybody was out, and no fire had broken out. The fire truck in trying to approach the plane got stuck in the mud. Fully loaded with water, it was just too heavy for the rain sodden soil to support. The hose would barely reach the aircraft. If it ran out of water it could do no more. It would have to go back to the station to get more water. Being stuck it couldn't go anywhere. Fortunately, no fire broke out.

As time wore on, Stan wondered about going back in the plane and getting his carry on stuff, but decided against it. He was standing out in the grassy field, observing the fire personnel trying to get the hose to the plane, and the plane lying like a crumbled model in some of the greenest grass on earth, except for the furrow of mud the plane had left in its wake. Stan also noticed the steam coming off the runway and grass from the latest passing shower. He didn't have a camera, but the picture in his mind was so surreal he would never forget it.

Later that night, Stan lay awake and thought about all the "what if..." and realized that he had just come close to serious injury or death. It took the ambulance well over 20 minutes to arrive and another 20 minutes to transport a few injured people to the hospital. One ambulance would not be enough to transport 10-20 people to the hospital if needed. Those that were injured would have some horrendous stories to tell about what happened when they got to the emergency room.

For a vacation in paradise, they had almost gone to the real paradise.

Exploding Battery

Stan had read about batteries exploding, but never gave it much thought. He was not aware of any practices he had when he jumped started a car or truck that would cause an explosion. What would cause a battery to explode anyway?

Frazer's brother, Martin, had a beat up old van that he was driving "for hire" on the road. The vehicle carried an "H" license plate. The "H" came at the beginning of the numbers on the license plate. You could tell when someone drove by if they were "for hire" (H) or "personal" (P) or a "truck" (T). He would drive routes from where he lived into Kingstown every day and try to pick up people to take to town. He wouldn't make much per person, but if he could stuff the van full of people, he would make more money.

Evidently Martin had a battery that was not holding a charge, and would put it on a battery charger at night. It generally would keep enough charge to start the engine in the morning.

The vehicle needed to be taken in for inspection, and before that, he needed a different set of tires. Generally van drivers didn't buy new tires; they would look for cheaper, used tires.

The road conditions being what they were, most tires did not last very long. There was a constant flow of used tires incoming to the island.

So one day found Stan on the bench seat behind the van driver. Martin was driving, and Frazer was on the passenger side. Stan had moved over to the center section so he could talk to both of them. The door to the battery compartment was lying on the floor. The battery compartment was located just behind the front passenger seat of the vehicle. The compartment door was off to make it easier to jump start the vehicle, or from leaving the battery charger on it overnight. The carpet that covered the compartment was lying down on top of the access hole.

They had stopped at a used tire place, and Martin had put on four tires. They sure looked better than the ones that were taken off. The old set of front tires were showing metal from the steel belt sticking through the rubber. Obviously Martin had worn them about as thin as you dared go.

When they went to drive off, the van had to be pushed to get it started, as the battery would not crank the engine. Now it was obvious that they couldn't shut the engine off, or they would have to push start it, or jump it to a good battery. So they drove down to the inspection station. It was getting close to lunch, and if they got there too late, they would have to come after the lunch hour.

They made sure that during the inspection the engine was not shut down. Much to Stan's surprise, the van passed inspection, and it was given a sticker that gave it clearance for the next year.

From there they drove to local car parts place for a battery. However, they arrived there just after 12 noon, and the place was closed. Frazer got on his phone and ordered lunch at an eatery nearby. They drove over to get their meal. Upon arrival they realized they would have to park the vehicle on a hill, so they could roll start it after they ate lunch.

As they were driving around looking for the best stopping place, the battery exploded with a very loud bang. Stan was wearing sunglasses and was very thankful for that. He felt the liquid from the battery spray his left side. Martin was not going fast and stopped almost instantly.

"Don't turn off the engine." Stan said as he climbed out of the van. Frazer came up with a bottle full of water and began pouring it over Stan's head and neck. Stan could taste the acid as he rinsed his face.

Stan recalled seeing out of the corner of his eye, the rug on top of the battery flying wide open, and then dropping back down on the battery. Later they would notice that all the plugs in the battery, used to fill it with water, were blown out, and scattered around the van. The handle to carry the battery was blown loose. The sides of the battery on two sides were gone, and you could see right into the battery. Most of the liquid went through a hole in the floor of the battery compartment.

After Stan rinsed his head and left arm, they dropped him off at the eatery. He went straight to the bathroom, and rubbed water everyplace he thought he had encountered acid. By now he had figured out that the sulfuric acid was pretty weak, which is one reason the battery would not hold a charge.

Martin took the van back to auto parts place and parked it on a hill. He walked back to the eatery for lunch.

They ate lunch, and they bought some baking soda and sprinkled it around the van and battery compartment. That would help neutralize the battery acid. They bought a new battery, and everything was ready to go. Later Stan was to notice that his shirt was stained as though it had been sprayed with Clorox; the bottom of his hat also had white spots on it. He now knew what it was like when a battery exploded, and he was thankful he did not suffer from any permanent injury from flying debris, or acid burns.

Chapter Ten

Beggars - Hurricanes – Finally - Almost Drowned

Stan and Marcy did not know what to do with the beggars. They were always around, and were always persistent. They were not sure they wanted to give because of some of the conversations with Frazer. They read in the newspaper that most of the beggars in town were on drugs. They were hesitant to help feed their habit. Probably one of the things that stopped them was the time they were in the bank and met one of the beggars making a deposit!

They began to say such phrases as "I don't have anything for you today." or "We give to people who we know that have a real need." This answered the question when beggars stuck out their hand and said, "Gimme a dalla." What they said was not a lie, and they didn't feel they were obligated to give to everyone who asked.

While there were beggars, they were thankful that pickpockets, purse snatchers and the like were virtually unknown. They would walk in town freely without fear of robbery, but the insistent beggars kept trying to get them to part with their money.

The beggars kept coming and their emotional stories kept changing. They would meet them carrying a letter saying they, or their children were in need of medical treatment. One letter sounded so good, but the date on the letter was over a year before.

Others had stamped papers with a place to put your name on a list to "support" them. You would sign and fill in how much you gave. That was what school children did for buying sports uniforms, and helping their special school functions. Counterfeit papers did circulate. Stan and Marcy decided, unless they knew the person, no cash money would be given.

Stan met some locals working on another sail boat that had obviously been sitting a long time in St. Vincent. The woodwork was ok, but badly in need of varnish work. The fiberglass was well worn and the keel had almost been snapped off.

They were working as funds became available. There were few tools around, and Stan thought "this is a project just like ours, maybe I could help. One day here with the right tools, and if they had the right parts, we could get a lot done." But as he looked around, he voiced no willingness to help directly, but did give lots of good advice.

Stan told them where his boat was and what they were doing on the island. Later he was to remember not seeing any form of transport around the boat, none. The two workers did not have a vehicle that Stan could see.

A week later Stan was working on the boat when Royken, from the nameless boat he had stopped at previously, called to him from outside the fence. Stan motioned for the security guard to let Royken in the gate, as he came down the ladder. He noticed the man with Royken had walked off towards the rum shop down the street. He was glad to show Royken the boat he was working on, and what he had done and what he intended to do. He proudly showed Royken where they had rebuilt the cabin and deck, but Royken had come with a different purpose in mind.

"I need some petrol." Royken explained.

When Stan realized this statement carried some sort of a question with it, and Royken was expecting an answer, he queried, "Petrol, for what?"

Royken explained, "My jeep ran out of petrol and I pushed it up on the side of the road. As I explained before, we sell vegetables and I was collecting some to take to the 12:00 ferry."

Stan vaguely knew the ferry schedule, and couldn't recall a 12:00 ferry.

"Where did you leave the jeep?" Stan asked as he was looking at his watch which said 11am.

It took some explaining but Royken kept at it until Stan had a mental picture of where the vehicle was. Not real close, but not all that far away. Royken had walked a fair distance. Stan knew there were no immediate gas stations near them or the vehicle, and none conveniently on the way.

Stan had given it some thought, and while he had not told Royken he would like to come and help them for a day, he decided this is one way to help them. He frankly told Royken that he believed his story. Beggars did not have a given address, and did not do hard work on boats.

Stan gave Royken some cold water to drink and carefully explained that he and Marcy had come to this conclusion that they did not hand out money to beggars. Royken replied that he really wasn't asking for money, he needed petrol. Stan had shown Royken all through the boat, and it was obvious as Stan pointed out, he didn't have petrol, and he wouldn't give any money.

As this dilemma was unfolding, Stan remembered that he had a gallon of petrol he had bought for the weed eater and he hadn't yet added oil to the gas. He then told Royken he had some gas, and he could go and put some petrol in his vehicle and then both could be on their way. Royken saw the plastic red tank, and commented that wasn't very much. Stan was sure a gallon would get Royken to town, and the ferry, and since Royken had mentioned going to the bank he could get some money and fill his tank. He noted that Royken wasn't looking too happy with the idea. But he knew it was the only solution he had.

"I need to go get my buddy. He's over at the shop." Royken said.

"Ok, let me climb back up and put some tools away, and shut the boat in case it rains. I'll meet you at the shop as it is in the direction we need to go to get to your vehicle." Stan replied.

Without waiting for a reply he started up the ladder and began gathering tools scattered on the deck. He noticed Royken outside the fence headed in the direction of the shop.

He put a few tools down below and shut and locked the hatch. That was his custom, just like he always locked his vehicle whenever he walked away from it. There was a security guard, and he knew him by name, and there was a fence around the place. But, he just locked the boat as he did any time he left it.

He got into the old truck and fired it up. At least it started. Then he eased out the gate and took a right turn. He did not see Royken, or the man in the orange shirt. He could see into the shop, and there were not many people inside. He pulled into the small parking area in front and waited, and waited, and waited some more. He looked into the shop carefully, and determined that Royken was not visible, nor his buddy. He was sure that by now they would have bought whatever they needed and come out by now. A quick jump out of the truck and a short walk to the shop door, and now he was sure, Royken was not inside, nor his buddy. They were not outside anywhere.

He immediately drove to where Royken said his vehicle was off the road. Just like Royken, the vehicle had also disappeared. Then he remembered not seeing a vehicle the first time he met Royken when he was working on the boat.

Stan laughed and smiled to himself all the way back to work on his boat. He couldn't wait to tell Marcy of the latest in how someone tried to con some money out of him.

Hurricane

One Saturday morning Stan and Marcy woke up to gusting winds and sheets of rain. Almost without warning, between Barbados and St. Vincent, a tropical wave had become a tropical depression, then a tropical storm, and was now classified as a hurricane. Less than twenty four hours from just a depression to a hurricane didn't leave much time to get out a hurricane warning. It didn't move much as it intensified. There were cloudy skies Friday evening. After it got dark it had turned to rain, and an ever increasing wind velocity. Nothing to indicate what was coming. Those who heard the warning were up late on Friday night. If they slept in, they would awaken to rising winds, and crashing waves.

Stan and Marcy had talked about what to do with a hurricane approaching, but were not prepared because of the quickness of the approaching storm. A hurricane is tracked by its eye; the eye is the center of the storm, where the winds swirl around in counter clockwise direction.

Stan immediately went to the boat, and began flooding the boat, figuring that by weighing more it would not fall over. He braced it with additional 2x4's. He had some tent stakes he drove into the ground and roped the boat down. He took down the awning, which was snapping in the wind.

His boat was located not very far from the sea's edge. There was nothing he could do if the sea flooded the land. He returned home, and the winds at times were very gusty. He quit driving at one point and stopped and felt the truck shudder from the wind. A nearby tree fell over.

When he got home, he was tired, and slept for a twenty minute power nap. Marcy was surprised that he would sleep when a hurricane was coming. But, Stan had noticed that the winds had let up momentarily as he approached the house. He calculated the eye was almost due north, and they had missed the most dangerous quadrant, the right hand front side of the hurricane. The winds in the right hand quadrant were the strongest. There the wind was not just the speed of the circling winds, but the speed of the forward motion of the hurricane added to make the total velocity greater. If you were in a boat, those winds would trap you, carry you around in the vortex, and finally out the back of the hurricane, prolonging your time in the winds.

If he faced the wind, the hurricane's center would be on the right hand. The wind had backed around from the usual direction of the north east trade winds, and was now blowing from due west. He couldn't find a radio station operating that had any real news on the center of the storm. His calculations were, the center was due north, which later proved to be true. For people in the digital age, that is a reference to the old timey watches/clocks that had hands that rotated towards the right as you faced the clock. The hurricane's winds were headed to the left of the hurricane vortex.

The only clear channel station operating that he could pick up was the Christian radio station out of Carriacou, Grenada, called *Harbour Light*. They had stayed on the air 24/7 when another hurricane, Ivan, hit directly on the Island of Grenada and stripped the roofs off 90% of the houses.

With the winds subsiding Stan estimated the eye was nearby. His rest ended when his wife woke him up and said he needed to be ready as the hurricane was here. He got up from the bedroom and walked into the living room. He glanced out the double glass door and watched a large tree go down. He now had a view of the nearby church that he couldn't see before. Finding that interesting, he grabbed a chair and sat in front of the glass door and propped his feet up on the glass. He could feel the glass tremor as gusts went by. He watched another tree topple. The glass door was parallel to the wind direction, and Stan didn't feel it was going to break.

"Shouldn't we have a contingency plan in case the roof comes off?" Marcy asked.

"Yes, I guess we should. Please get me my shoes from the bedroom." Stan replied.

Marcy then asked if they should be boarding up windows, or the door. Stan didn't reply as he was watching the galvanized peel off the roof of the house across the street. Frazer's house was on a slight hill. The house was sheltered by two houses slightly taller than his, and Stan felt safe watching the gusts as they shook the trees.

At the end of the storm Frazer's house was undamaged, as were most homes. There were some houses up on the mountain side that had their roofs peel off. But as the wind settled down, the owners retrieved the galvanized and soon the sound of hammers echoed around the hills.

Probably every banana tree was leveled on the island. That was the main income for the island and it was going to take awhile to recover from the damage.

The wind was the minimum for a hurricane, at about 75 mph and gusting to 90. Stan had seen this kind of wind, though not from a hurricane. While out racing yachts on an Annapolis-Newport ocean race a northeaster hit the fleet. The event was back in the Coast Guard Days, and the he was on a Coast Guard boat racing from Annapolis to Newport News, Rhode Island. They were warned before setting out. Just when and where the storm would hit was unknown. Down Chesapeake Bay was a summer's cruise. Winds were light and variable. The bigger yachts seemed to find wind up higher on their masts and were leaving the shorter masted boats becalmed. At times, it seemed as if the neat thing to do would be to drop the sails and jump overboard for an inviting swim. They sailed south down the bay and then turned out to sea for the Chesapeake light. They were to pass the lighthouse close by and identify themselves so the race organizers would at least know who got this far along in the race. The lighthouse was only partly automated, and had residents. It stood on steel stilts several miles offshore.

Later, Stan found out that the other yacht, *Manitou*, from the Academy, had an interesting experience when rounding the tower. Their safety officer had all hands on deck as they meandered through the lobster traps, and sand bars that dotted the Chesapeake Bay. When they finally entered the open ocean he set watches as the duty crew hardened the boat up on the northeast wind and headed for the checkpoint at the light tower.

For privacy sake we will call him Ed. Ed went to sleep thinking he would get four hours before being called on deck to take his turn at sailing. After 18 hours of being on deck, Ed was grateful to get four hours of sleep before he would be awakened to sail the yacht. While in a deep sleep, *Manitou* neared the light tower. It was now night and the navigation lights on the tower were on. *Manitou* was darkened, and had just the running lights, and compass light lit. Within less than a hundred yards a big booming voice came from the light tower, "Who are you?" There were several boats in the area and the tower was using a powerful spotlight, shining it onto the sails looking for ID numbers.

Ed awoke with a start when he heard the booming voice. *Manitou* had a skylight right above the mid-ships bunks where he was laying. There was a bright light shining through. He was sure it was the Lord calling his name. He could see nobody else in their bunks because of the light shining through the skylight had blinded him. His eyes were not accustomed to the dark. Then he heard the voice the second time "Who are you?" He jumped out of bed and headed for the companion way. Scared, alone (he thought), and the light from the companion way blinding him, he was sure the Lord had come for him. He could barely discern the steps in the companion way leading to the cockpit.

He gained the cockpit and looked right up into the spotlight. He was disoriented from being awakened from deep sleep, and with the light in his eyes tripped and fell into the cockpit. Again, with his eyes blinded by the light, he couldn't see any one in the cockpit, and in a state of fear he heard the voice again, "Who are you?"

Convinced he was alone and facing judgment from Almighty God, he got to his knees and began confessing his sins and repenting, out loud. He was interrupted by gales of laughter from the gang sitting in the cockpit wondering what was going on!! Then they informed him, it was just the light from the lighthouse, and their megaphone he heard wanting to know the identity of *Manitou*. It was not God calling for him! His "repentance" only lasted until they got into port and he headed for the closest bar.

Stan's boat rounded the tower later on, and had no problems. The next day in daylight they could see a squall coming that was dark and ominous. Sail was reduced before it arrived, and when it did, it began to blow. Eventually building to 90 mph winds with 30 foot seas.

When Stan was sleeping down below he could tell if an experienced helmsman was steering or a newby. The uninformed drove straight into the oncoming wave, and while the wave was somewhat gentle with its breaking foam, the backside of the wave didn't exist. There would be an almost 30 foot plunge down the backside of the wave. An experienced helmsman kept the windward course as close into the wave as he could, and then at the top of the wave turn off to leeward, and surf down the backside of the vertical wave.

This went on for hours. Eventually, you had to find a way to sleep. Stan was in a pipe rack in the bow, and had a mattress on bottom of the rack, and one on top of him. The mattress on the top provided a cushion when the boat plunged down. An inexperienced helmsman would drive directly across the wave and the boat would fall into the trough. That made his body slam into the overhead. He had put life jackets all around the berth, to keep him padded from the pipe that formed the frame of the canvas pipe berth, and from the side of the yacht.

Occasionally the waves on deck would find a crack in the seal for the forward hatch, and rain into the bed on the leeward side.

Meals were suspended and people ate what they could eat. Once when a crew didn't come up for duty, Stan slid the hatch and observed two guys eating corn beef straight out of the can. When that ran out they looked for other non cooking nourishment. There had been a mix-up when the yachts were provisioned, and Stan's yacht ended up with two big boxes of Hershey chocolate bars. That provided the nourishment for a couple of days.

Stan found out that the boat would sail in 90 mph winds, with just the storm jib flying. The only "structural" damage was done when someone dropped a shackle overboard.

Finally!

After several months of very hot and hard work it came time to launch. They had informed Al that they had finished this phase of work, and were more than ready to move onto the next step. Stan was getting nervous; the longer they delayed, the more "into" hurricane season they would be.

But launching day came bright and clear, as most days had become. The wind was out of the North east as it had blown for generations. Their launch down a simple ramp would not be that easy, but they had faith in the expertise of Frazer. "No problem boss, we pulled it up, we can get it back in."

The crane arrived late to pick the boat up and swing it over to the rail. But they had already planned on that and told the operator to come two hours early. So they were actually on time. The crane operator hoisted the boat high into the air, and the wind became a factor as one of the gusts that shoots down off the mountain hit and made the whole rig sway in the breeze. But the crane swung the boat around, and deposited it on the trolley, ready for the ride to the water. Before the boat was slid into the water, the same crane helped step the mast after the customary silver dollar was put on the mast step. There were a couple of places on the hull where the jack stands and wood had prevented the hull from being painted with anti-fouling paint, something very needful in the tropical waters. Stan had paint brush in hand and was slapping on the last of the anti-fouling paint as the boat slid slowly down the railway into the water.

A few minutes later, and the boat was in the water and they were ready to begin moving aboard. Most things were already on the boat as they had watched this procedure for other boats and realized *Susan* was smaller and lighter than most boats that graced the ways of Frazer's yard.

There was a short stop at the dock at the "rent-a-yacht" place (changed names and owners every few years) for water and ice and the last minute things they needed. Then they were ready for the short shakedown cruise.

They sailed the channel between Bequia and St. Vincent. It had short choppy seas, but not very rough as the wind was not very strong. There they cruised down to Tobago Cays, the gem of the Caribbean. They found the water crystal clear and large fish swimming, just as it was when they had come earlier. It was just like a giant aquarium, only there was no glass between them and the wild life.

It is considered one of the dive spots in the Caribbean. No permanent structures are allowed on the islands, anchorages were only allowed in designated areas. Fishing, whether by line or spear, is strictly forbidden.

One day while snorkeling, a shark went swimming by. While the shark got larger every time they told the story, it couldn't have gotten any closer. Reaching out and touching it was a possibility, but it was one thing they did not attempt. Turning and swimming away was also on option they did not use. They didn't want to leave their feet stuck out for him to munch on. Instead they did a backwards crab movement watching the shark swim out of sight into the distance. They were done with swimming for that day! They were embarrassed when people asked them what kind of shark it was, they didn't have a clue.

These were the days they had dreamed about while commuting through the snow. They were amazed that it actually was happening. Blue skies, blue seas, sailing wind blowing, no job to get back to, supplies to last awhile, and not a care in the world. It had made all the work worthwhile.

After a few days of exploring the area, they decided to return to St. Vincent and offer Frazer and his family a ride out on the boat.

They doubled back and spent some time at Admiralty Bay in Bequia. Everybody was friendly and many yachtsmen gathered in the bay. They realized that Bequia was one of the best spots in the Caribbean.

Peter's Hope

Almost drowned

Stan and Marcy returned to St. Vincent, and stocked up on groceries and other last minute needed items. The list was fairly extensive, but they were going to be leaving and were unsure of prices in other islands.

They contacted Frazer and excitedly told him how things were going and they wanted him to bring his whole family out to the boat.

Frazer informed them that he was not interested in going to sea. While he worked constantly with boats, any excursion on the rough waters, he got sea sick. They eventually worked out a compromise where he would bring his whole family to Mount Wynne on Saturday, and the kids could swim off the boat.

Stan and Marcy immediately set sail for the leeward side of the island. Most anchorages were sandy, and even though the Caribbean Sea lay to the west of them in open environment, they felt secure. The wind came from the land side and was blowing them out to sea. The anchor kept them secure. If it drug on the bottom, or the anchor line broke, they would be blown into deeper water, not up on the beach. One Friday night they anchored in Mt. Wynne bay and looked forward to the Frazer's coming the next day.

On Saturday Stan woke up to small ripples on the surface, a nice wind blowing over the top of the trees and mountains, but everything was secure. The anchor was about 15 feet down and dug into soft sand. They had not moved during the night and the anchor had held them very nicely. Because of the ripples on the surface, he couldn't see clearly to the bottom, but the fathometer said 15 feet.

Marcy was still sleeping as he dived over the side into the blue waters. The visibility past the surface ripples was great. He could see over a hundred yards in any direction. This was what all the work and labor was for. On the bottom of the lagoon he saw a trolling lure. It looked closer, but he knew that distances were deceiving.

He jackknifed into the water, and headed for the bottom. At about 13 feet he cleared his ears by pinching his nose and blowing. He reached down and picked up the lure. It looked brand new. He carefully held it by the stainless steel leader, as he was afraid of the large double hooks buried in the purple looking octopus. He tugged on the leader and found out that the line led over to the rocks nearby, but it was stuck. Not wanting to push his time on the bottom he dropped the lure and swam to the surface. He kicked over to the rocks and looked around, but the line was transparent in the water. He went back to the lure and went to the bottom to see if he could pick it up again. As he was just off the stern of his boat he felt no danger, he carried no knife, and was of course not using the buddy system as Marcy was still catching up on her sleep.

This time he picked up the lure and gave it a tug and was surprised to feel it come loose from its entanglement. He headed for the surface with his prize in tow. This would be a nice souvenir of their journey. Maybe even a useful one, as it could be towed off the stern. About half way to the surface he felt the line tighten as it tangled again on the bottom. Quicker than he could do anything, his hand slid down almost a foot of the stainless steel leader and he hooked his finger. He was not aware of the pain, but he was aware that the surface was still 7 feet away and he wasn't going to reach it. His immediate thought was that he hadn't said good bye to his wife, and that when she woke up, she would find the body easily enough, right off the back of the boat still attached to this fishing line.

At first he tried to use his other hand to pull the hook out of the finger, but already the hook was past the barb into his finger, and it would not come free. Without a knife he couldn't cut it, and even though he wasn't yet feeling like he was running out of air he knew that feeling was coming soon enough. Forever etched in his mind was the thought that he had a good idea what a fish felt when it went once too often for the bait. Before he lost all momentum to the surface he did the only thing he knew to do. In a near panic he kicked with his fins and pulled with all that he could. The hook sank even deeper into his finger but fortunately he felt the line come free off the bottom. He swam to the surface with his prize embedded into his finger. As he came up the swim ladder in the back of the boat, Marcy stuck her head over the transom.

"How's the water?"

"The water is great"

"See anything?"

"Saw lots of things."

"Think I'll come in."

"Well, before you do that, let me come out." As he hoisted himself up on the boat, he said, "I think swimming is over for now." as he showed Marcy his finger impaled on the hook.

They got in the dinghy and Marcy rowed him to the shore. Frazer showed up on the beach at this very opportune time. He drove them to the hospital in town. Over the winding roads it took 35 minutes before they reached the hospital. Of course there never is an emergency, and the doctor was not due in for another hour.

The night before, in the emergency room, had been long. They were busy stitching up some late night revelers who had traded blows and slashes with beer bottles at Carnival.

The doctor numbed his finger, and cut out the hook. It was embedded in such a way they couldn't push it on through, past the barbs, and cut off the ends. It took four stitches to seal up the wound. Stan had a souvenir that he would have the rest of his life. He had a good idea of how helpless a fish feels, and realized just how close their vacation in paradise had about ended with him facing eternity and wondering about the real place called paradise. Death is a persistent stalker.

Instead of heading back to the boat immediately, Marcy cajoled him into going into town and eating breakfast.

Later that night he was sitting on the boat and thinking about how close to death he had come. Marcy came over and gave him a hug, and he hugged her back and just cried.

Bequia Regatta

Chapter Eleven

Collision at Sea – Survival – Adrift – Starting Over
(A collision at sea can ruin your whole day)

Stan and Marcy had to wait around a few days until the doctor removed the stitches. Stan's hands were so important for handling sails and lines. The skin is subject to blisters and cuts. In salt water, blisters would easily rip open. Infection sets into the sore. The salt water prevents the wound from healing. They could not risk his stitches to re-open. It was two more weeks before they set sail.

On such a small boat a week makes a difference, as there is not room enough to store much food onboard. So they made another trip to Kingstown with a list of necessary items. They then decided to go over to Bequia and spend a couple of days, walking the island. That led to one more trip down to Tobago Cays and Union Island. The wind and sea and sun were glorious, and this was what they wanted to do. Marcy had to learn how to handle the boat herself as Stan was very cautious to use the damaged hand.

They finally set sail north, with a light northeasterly wind. Even though they were still in the ending of the hurricane season, they had not really checked the weather, and there was no talk among the yachties that such a storm was approaching.

They set a course up the leeward side of St. Vincent towards Dominica. However, the wind was light and they drifted off towards the west with the current. Night fell and they were several miles offshore when the squall line moved in. Knowing this was no hurricane, they had not contemplated what a "wave", and turning to tropical storm could do, especially if it stalled in their area. If a storm stalls in movement, it generally grows bigger and angry. They can become hurricanes. They were soon traveling with just the storm jib, and the course had set them farther offshore and to the west. The next day greeted them with an endless row of whitecaps and driving rain. Marcy was not feeling well, Stan was in his element and enjoyed staying on deck and yelling whenever a big wave came rolling by.

Stan was sure of his handiwork, and since much of the rigging was either new, or recently inspected, he knew that they could weather most storms. Size is not always a sign of strength. A cargo ship would have to have a hull several inches thick of steel, to be as strong as *Susan*'s hull was for the length. A bottle with a good stopper on it can ride out a storm. The occupant may get shaken around a little.

The wind had shifted rather rapidly to the south, and Stan began to be concerned that the storm instead of lessening was strengthening. He dropped the storm jib and lashed it down. The sea anchor was set, and they began a slow drift. They were tethered to the sea anchor and drifting backwards slowly towards the north while the bow was facing the south.

The sea anchor is like a small parachute deployed underwater. It attaches to the boat by a single line. A swivel allows it to twist and turn without kinking the rope. If properly deployed, it will hold a boat steady in a position facing the wind and waves. It is not attached to the bottom. Wind driven current, tidal current, sea currents, will all play into which way the boat will drift. The sea anchor just lets the boat face the waves and wind.

Nightfall came and there seemed no relief or letup in the wind or the waves.

Stan had gone up on deck to check the boat. Seas were not that big at 8' but their fetch gave no chance for rest, and made for a complete lack of comfort. Marcy was still slightly seasick but okay. She was not in the mood to cook, or to eat. She was lying on the port bunk. She had rigged a canvas preventer: a square piece of canvas screwed under the length of the mattress, and tied to the side of the boat. It formed something like a hammock, which prevented her from being dumped on the floor, if there was a sudden lurch of the boat. She had tied a bucket near her head, within easy reach - "just in case."

With the wind from the south, Stan began to realize they might be in for some rough weather for awhile. An "almost a hurricane" had practically formed on top of them without too much warning. It would eventually blow by them, but they were not sure how long it would take. No sails, tiller tied down, out of the normal transit lanes, they were just bobbing up and down with the sea anchor holding them in position.

The boat was headed SSE, but drifting north with the current. They wanted to work their way back towards the islands, instead of being blown further into the Caribbean Sea. But, they were at the mercy of the wind and waves. Wind and sea were there main concerns, and a 26' boat was not powerful enough to make much headway. He could not set sail until the wind dropped. Then it promised to be a wet beat to windward to any nearby island.

Marcy was down below, almost out of action, it left Stan the only one to really manage the boat. They didn't mind being blown so far into the Caribbean Sea; it was going to be just easier to let the wind blow them around. They had plenty of sea room, and were just holding their own. In the next 24 hours this storm would be history, they hoped, and they could shake out the reef and begin to get to the next island.

Stan went to the mast so he could see the shine of the running lights, and was sighting up the mast to check it out for any signs of flexing. The small engine in *Susan* would be of little value in these conditions, and they would need the sails to set a course that would take them back to land. If the mast was bending too much, Stan would have to tighten the appropriate stays.

Stan began studying how *Susan* was taking the waves. The sea anchor was about two waves to windward and holding well. The boat was not backing down or slewing sideways with the passing waves. Either condition would be hard on the rudder.

It was tied amidships and if *Susan* slid backward it could put enough pressure on the rudder to break it. He was looking aft and studying the rudder motions when they were hit by a wave. He heard a noise to windward. He turned and looked and there was this aluminum beam coming over the waves straight at him! His reflex was to jump and when he came down he hit neither the deck of his own boat, nor the water, but landed in a net and tumbled over and over. He had not seen a light of any passing ship the entire time he had come up on deck. He had no idea what had just happened.

Even with the screeching of the wind he could hear some major crashing and thumping going on. He could hear Marcy screaming but couldn't figure out where. In fact he wasn't sure where he was. When he stopped rolling he realized he was lying on this large net and there were some unfamiliar voices screaming around him. He had landed on the front deck of a very large catamaran, and evidently they had passed right over the top of his boat and had hardly slowed down.

As the catamaran climbed a wave he could see over the stern of the cat. His boat was minus the mast and most of the cabin top. It was still on the sea anchor with the wake of the catamaran straddling its position. He had changed boats and he could see that there was no way to get back to his. And he had no idea where this one was heading.

Then he saw I-See, the Rastafarian. There was no mistaking that scar across his face. He also recognized Dave from the airplane trip several months ago. They didn't recognize him with his long beard, and very tan body. He figured out he was in trouble more than one way.

The mast from *Susan* was bent and twisted lying across the tramp of the catamaran. The cat's forestay looked very loose, and the front beam had bent. They had a small storm jib set. Somebody switched on the cross tree lights and in the rain and spray the cat took on a surreal appearance. Stan couldn't believe what had happened. Then he heard the surprised voices of the crew when they realized they had a new passenger. He immediately began shouting to drop the jib, or their mast would be coming down.

Frantically Stan went to the jib and began tugging at it, yelling to lose the sheet to relieve the pressure on the mast. He realizes now that instinct to save the boat probably saved his life, as the crew of three didn't really know how to handle the boat. Instead of trying to kill him, they began easing the sheet, and dropping the halyard until they had some kind of control on the sail. Fortunately they had left sail ties on the pulpit and lifelines forward, and he used them to tie down the sail.

The men were not happy to see him, but he was quickly pointing out that the forestay was obviously loose and the mast could be in danger of falling. When back in the cockpit and all was settled down, Stan explained how he got on their boat, and the concern he had for his boat, and for his wife. He mentioned seeing *Susan* bobbing in their wake, minus the mast and cabin top. While he was talking, Stan was looking around.

Stan had been noticing several things that bothered him, but made no comment on. He noticed the pistol that Dave wore, and though he had never been around drug runners before; he began to figure it out. He figured that the boat was running drugs north, and he was an unwilling participant! He knew then that his life was on the line. Everything he did could only prolong his life, as it just might be forfeited.

While he had tanned and grew a beard while working on *Susan*, Ben and Dave still looked as they did, the day they stepped off the plane in Barbados.

So he took charge of the situation.

"That mast will not take the pressure of setting sails. It needs to be stabilized before it comes free. Ever stepped a mast before?"

"No." Each one answered.

"Could I show you how?"

"We sure need it. We don't have enough fuel to motor to Puerto Rico." Said Dave.

"Do you have any non stretch rope onboard?" Stan queried. He asked where they had any extra rope on board, preferably non-stretch.

With the main furled, they kept the cat on its downward course, taking the strain off the forestay. Stan explained that they were going to use the spare halyard to pull the non stretch rope to the top of the mast. The non stretch rope would be secured directly to one of the bows. They would use the halyard winch to tighten up this temporary forestay. Hopefully enough tension could be taken to take the pressure of the Genoa and main. While he was talking, he was also trying to figure out a way to get off the boat alive.

177

Stan noticed the high speed dinghy on the back of the boat sitting in a davit. It was a RIB with a high powered engine and built in gas tanks. He figured out rightly that everything around him was stolen. It was on a one way trip to Puerto Rico and then would be abandoned. The storm had probably kept most boats in harbor in this tropical paradise, and the fewer boats around, the better their chances of not being detected.

They produced some line and Stan sent Ben to the bow to tie it off. He gave I-See the job of winching it tight. The halyard leads back to the cockpit so Dave and I-See were there together. Stan was back in the cockpit to see if it pulled the mast to far over to one side. Ben began the journey to the bow.

Dave was steering the boat and sometimes turned his back to protect himself from the spray. They were not counting on Stan to try anything. Stan lurched against Dave steering the boat. He actually slipped the gun out of Dave's holster and had moved away before anyone noticed that he had it. By then he was already moving towards I-See and made him back away from the self-tailing halyard winch. As he passed the winch I-See had already tightened up, Stan pulled out his knife that was sheathed just below his knee. Stan always carried on a knife on his person when on board a boat. He cut the line. They would have to re-rig it, giving him more time.

Ben up on the bow noticed the line went slack and began yelling to pull tighter. He did not know what was happening in the cockpit. When he pulled to tighten, the now free end of the halyard started up the mast, and every foot it went up, there was an equal weight of rope on the other side pulling it down.

Eventually the halyard pulled through the top pulley on the mast, and fell on the deck.

With the adrenaline pumping, Stan cut the ropes holding the dinghy free and spun it over the side. He sheaved the knife, jammed the gun in his belt and did a flip into the dinghy.

Getting back to the engine he was surprised at how fast the cat was moving away from him. Even without a sail up, it was coasting down sea very fast. He noticed that Dave had disappeared from the cockpit, and about the time he got the engine started Dave was back on deck and he heard the unmistakable sound of an M-16 opening up on him. With one hand steering and one hand shooting he quickly moved away from them as he returned fire. The range was not all that great but in both cases, the heaving sea made it very difficult to aim. Dave may have been a good shot on land, but it is a lot more difficult on a moving, heaving boat. Dave also ducked when Stan returned fire, which gave Stan even more time and distance, and in an 8' wave he was easily behind the wave and finding protection in the trough. It is one thing to have target practice; it is entirely different when the target is shooting back! Dave was afraid of getting shot. Stan was fearful also, but he knew he had to get back to Marcy. He stood up and carefully squeezed off each shot, and he could hear them hitting somewhere on the deck of the catamaran. The darkness and rain swallowed him up.

He got more distant as he began heading up wind. He was sure it would be awhile before they could come looking for him in the cat, if at all. They would have to re-rig the line he cut, and then turn up into the wind. A little fearful of whether or not it would really work might keep them heading north and forgetting about him.

While he was no longer sure exactly where *Susan* and his wife were, they had to be upwind of the catamaran. While *Susan* was holding her own on the sea anchor, the cat was going downwind. He headed south, against the wind and sea.

In all, over an hour had elapsed, and when they disappeared from sight, he seemed to be alone on the sea. He knew that the distances were not that great and if the druggies came looking for them, he would be in serious trouble. Daylight would shed a whole different light on the situation, and he only had a couple of bullets left in the gun, while the druggies were obviously well armed.

Survival

Marcy was half sleeping and half awake down below. This dream vacation had turned into a nightmare, only she was not sleeping. She began to see this was going to be an endurance contest and she wasn't sure if she was able to go on with this. Her stomach had not rejected her last try at eating, but she wasn't really sure if it could hold any more food at all. Add to that the dry taste in her mouth, and the slight head ache, she was not feeling well. Of course the movement of the boat had been very tiring, and she was glad that Stan had figured out a way to make the boat steer itself, and she was not needed on deck to stand a watch.

In her half sea sick state she wasn't keeping track of time, but knew that Stan had stepped out on deck to check the boat. She was aware of a terrible sound of the something colliding with another. At first she didn't know what it was. The first thing to go was the forestay and that sounded like a loud gun going off where she lay. Her tiredness and feelings let her linger in bed for an instant which may have saved her life.

The next sound was the collision of the forward beam of the cat as it tore off the cabin top. If she had stood up, her head would have been in the way of the aluminum beam as it ate off the top of the cabin, and finished off the mast as it toppled over. Her slight case of sea sickness had saved her life.

Then *Susan* was under the bridge of the cat and Marcy was on her knees looking up as the cat passed over the top of the boat. It was hitting and sliding as it went by, then the view was of darkness and the rain began to hit her in the head. She stood up and as the motion of the boat allowed, she could look out the cabin top and see the big cat as it moved swiftly away into the darkness. There were no visible lights on the catamaran. Then just before it disappeared into the inky depths of dark night, the spreader lights came on and she could see its towering mast. But, the speed of the cat, and the size of the waves quickly made it disappear.

Fear almost took complete control of the boat. She didn't know where Stan was, and she didn't really know how the collision had occurred, and she wasn't sure what she should do next with no mast and no cabin top. At first she was just yelling and screaming for Stan, and almost went into hysteria when she realized he was not around. She was shaking, and she didn't know if it was from crying or from the cold driving rain.

She put on a life jacket, which gave her some protection from the cold. Since she had lain down in her foul weather gear she really wasn't all that wet, only where the seams leaked water.

The boat without the mast and the cabin top became more stable in the water. The motion of the boat quieted, which gave her a chance to gather her thoughts and strength. The sea anchor was holding. The wind had begun to abate.

Marcy climbed out on the deck, and on her hands and knees while crying softly, her salty tears mixing with the ocean spray, she surveyed the damages. The cabin top was sheared away, and the mast was gone, along with any of the sails attached to it. At this point she knew that she was on her own. She was sure Stan was not on the boat and she had no idea if he was in the water, had been hurt in the collision or what. Not just shock, but grief and fear were crowding into her thoughts.

Marcy began to have her stomach unknot, and she began to realize her predicament. She was not sure of where she was, the engine could not be used in these large waves, there was not a mast to put sails on, and she didn't know where Stan was. With the sea anchor out, *Susan* was slowly drifting down wind, down sea, backwards, facing the incoming waves. *Susan* was slowly drifting north.

She went back "down below", which really wasn't down below anymore because there wasn't a cabin top. It was all open to the wind and waves, and the rain was still coming down in torrents. When she stepped on the cabin sole, she had noticed that the floor boards in the boat were floating. The adrenaline was still pumping and she was not even aware of how she got to the cockpit at all. Did she climb the three steps up the ladder into the cockpit, or did she just jump up? She immediately began to pump on the bilge pump and in 53 strokes pumped the bilge dry. Stan had told her to count the strokes when she pumped. If she had to do it again she may note that there was a leak, and if it was getting worse.

She decided that her next step would be to cover what she could of the cabin top to keep out the rain and spray. She was fortunate that the waves were not breaking over the deck of the boat. It was high sided in its design, and had been lightened several hundred pounds with the removal of the cabin top, mast and Stan.

She went back below and retrieved a flashlight. A check of the bilge confirmed they were almost dry. She was not sure how much would accumulate as the heavy rain continued to fall. She knew she would build a cabin top out of whatever she could find. The largest sail now left on the boat was the Ginny that had been stuffed into the forepeak when they got into the storm and set the storm jenny. She wasn't going to need it any time soon, so she nailed it down over the cabin top which stopped most the rain coming in. As she finished that job she tried some more pulls on the bilge pump and counted 20 strokes to get the water out.

She was not sure of how much time had elapsed but she felt that she now could survive, despite her fears. She also realized that she hadn't even thought about being seasick since the cabin top had been ripped off. Now that the adrenaline was wearing out she found herself hungry. She went below and under the protection of the jenny stretched across the gaping hole; she found some crackers and a can of Pepsi. A look at her watch let her know that daylight would come in about two hours. She checked the bilge and noticed there was more water there, but not much.

Marcy climbed back up into the cockpit and was relieved to find that only ten strokes emptied the bilges. She went down below and attempted to get some sleep. She set an alarm every hour to wake her. She wanted to check the bilge.

It was daylight and the boat seemed to be riding very smoothly when she awoke at 10 AM. She had slept right through the alarm. The bilge was awash, but not any worse than she had seen the night before. She went up and pumped them dry, 20 strokes.

Back below, Marcy figured out that while most everything was wet, the stove still worked. She cooked up some eggs and found a way to heat up the bread into a semblance of a toast; after eating she felt better. The rain had stopped, the seas were a little quieter, and the sun was out. She began to hope that she was going to survive. Things were looking better, and the wind seemed to be moderating.

But there were no boats in sight; she still had no idea of where she was much less an idea of how to get anywhere. The engine was still an enigma of how it worked, and she judged the seas to steep and too big for it to work very well.

When the cabin top had been ripped off the radio that was so convenient to the passageway had gone with it. She did find the flare kit in the foul weather gear locker. She calculated she had several weeks of food, and plenty of water. She was in a big ocean with a small boat, and no clue as to how to get to shore.

Marcy also did not know what had happened to Stan. She decided to lie down again as the visibility was not very good, the boat was doing fine and there was nothing else to do.

Adrift at Sea

It was the voice that really got her attention. At first she just heard the shout, and then she thought she recognized the voice, and then finally in her grogginess she realized she had heard Stan. But how was that possible?

She jumped up and with three quick steps, she could see over what was left of the cabin top and was trying to locate the voice. Even though she still thought maybe she was hearing things she shouted a reply.

She did not know how it could be Stan!! But she continued to yell, and then heard a reply. Then she got a whistle off the life jacket and began to blow.

Over to her right she thought she saw something before it went into the trough of a wave. The wind had quit, but the waves were still around eight-ten feet but were now gentle rollers. Then as the waves rolled a little farther she saw a small boat. It only had one occupant, who she couldn't yet identify, but it was headed straight for her and the person was waving.

Within just a few minutes it became obvious it was Stan. Somehow he was here. It brought up lots of questions, how did he get a dinghy, how did he find her here? She jumped up on top of the seats of the cockpit and continued to wave, not taking her eyes off the boat as the distances closed.

It was Stan!! He was alive!! It was a real thrill.

The boat bumped alongside and Stan threw her the painter. She quickly tied it to the cleat and he leaped the distance separating the boats and they were in each other's arms. He quickly explained of his ordeal the night before, and miraculous escape. He had guessed at her location and distance, and done an S pattern coming against the wind and waves. Finding her though, was another miracle as both his dinghy and what was left of *Susan* was low to the water. With seas over 10 feet, they could have missed each other so easily.

He went into what was left of the galley and cooked up a quick meal of bacon and eggs. He got her to start packing food, fishing gear, and anything else they would need.

They transferred all the gas/oil for *Susan's* engine onto the dinghy. The outboard was running on fumes. Stan thought that if the big cat came looking for them the best chance of escape was with the powerboat. It was faster and lower in the water.

He assumed if he could find *Susan*, so could they, and if they stayed on *Susan* they would be sitting ducks.

He even took the jenny and a couple of pieces of wood and oars thinking that he could maybe even rig a sail if necessary. Land, but not necessarily safety, lay to the east of their position.

Stan took one last look around to see if there was anything else he could take with him. He actually took the time to pump the bilges dry before he stepped into the power boat. Little did he know what was going to be important in the future. The rain had quit by the time they had loaded the boat.

About the time they got the dinghy loaded up, they noticed a sail on the horizon. They jumped into the boat, and he took a course that would open the distance between them and the sail boat. They did not want to encounter the people on that large cat. They were not even sure if this was the large catamaran.

With gas from their boat Stan calculated that they could head east and hopefully encounter a windward island. He had brought some charts and a compass, and anything he thought he could use.

Not familiar with the most efficient cruising speed of the dinghy, he figured on using about ½ throttles. The waves and wind made it somewhat easy to set an easterly course without having to consult the hand held compass too often. After all, it spun somewhat in the wave action, and with all the metal cans, and whatever was around the compass he wasn't sure of its accuracy, but it seemed to check out with what looked good.

The waves seemed to be abetting, and the wind was almost gone. Stan knew that the worst that could befall them was being found by the people on the cat. He knew that they would not like him leaving, or taking the dinghy. He also somehow knew that his knowledge of the weed (marijuana) on board would not be something that they wanted Stan to share with anyone.

He also had a suspicion that the boat was probably stolen and was being used for a drug haul, and then would be abandoned. So a vigilant look-out was necessary, not just to steer the boat, but to watch for sails. Marcy was fully recovered from any twinge of sea sickness, and willing to steer and do whatever was necessary.

He was now beginning to think that there would be other problems. They had logged out of St. Vincent, but were not sure just how immigration would take to him showing up with another boat, without proper ID for the boat he now had.

The culprits had painted a new name and new ID ready for the big cat, but they hadn't yet painted over the name on the dinghy, which had the name on the side of a boat that would be reported stolen. He kept moving at what he hoped was an optimum speed and headed for what he hoped was land.

Thinking about the Windward Islands, one would know they were all volcanic in nature and most over 4,000 feet high. If it was not cloudy Stan expected to see an island from over 60 miles away. As most were about 20-40 miles apart, he assumed that he would see one of the islands before passing through a pass between islands and entering the Atlantic. At least that was the plan. Presently spray, lingering clouds and occasional light rain obscured the horizon.

Late afternoon it began to snow! Or so they thought. It was just lightly coming down, but it slowly settled over the entire dinghy. It was a gray colored snow that defied description. They began to realize that it wasn't really snow as it wasn't cold, but they could not identify this substance. They later found out that Montserrat volcano had erupted and what they thought was snow was actually volcanic ash.

It made things very slippery on the boat. At first they worked on cleaning it up, but gave up as it continued to settle. They did notice that the horizon stayed murky and visibility was poor. Darkness settled in and they took turns steering east and slightly south

By 10 PM they were sure that the lights they were seeing were on land. They changed course to head straight for them. Despite Marcy's objections, Stan kept off shore. He was looking for geographical indications as to where they were. Eventually they were close enough to shore, and the "snow" had also stopped, they saw a geographical reference point.

Stan noticed the Grand Pitons just south of their position, and without chart or map knew exactly where he was, and where he wanted to go. They were two twin mountains on the western side of St. Lucia. He crept up close to land and killed the engine. The drift was negligible. He needed to rest, and wanted to wait until daylight to enter port. He could also avoid paying an extra "after hours" fee.

Since they had their passports, credit cards, and paperwork for *Susan* they decided to put into St. Lucia for fuel. They check in with customs and asked for 24 hour stay, to clear when they had refueled and refurbished. They decided to tell no one in St. Lucia their problem, and hopefully get back to St. Vincent. Their fuel supply was less than a gallon, and Stan was pretty sure that was not enough to get to St. Vincent. They went to the police station to clear customs. The police never looked out the window to see what boat was really out there. He stamped their papers and welcomed them to St. Lucia.

They topped up their fuel tanks, and went out to eat. They cleared when they were ready and got back into the dinghy/speedboat and headed for St. Vincent as fast as they could make time. Their destination was Howard's Marina. They had quite a story to tell to Frazer and needed to call Al.

Starting all Over

Stan and Marcy after consulting with Frazer decided to tell the Coast Guard of their misadventure. Reports were filed, and forgotten as far as they could tell. However, Al had used the Coast Guard report to contact his insurance company, who confirmed the *Susan* as presumed lost at sea.

Not much time elapsed before questions were answered as to their next step. Marcy had decided that they had survived, and challenges were not to go unheeded. Plus with each challenge, they learned something new about life. Stan had found some new confidence in making quick decisions. They had come to the Caribbean to do things that other people were afraid to do. They came to enjoy life, and while there had been some bumps and obstacles, they had enjoyed the thrill.

They were down at Canash bay not far from where *Susan* was launched; sitting on the sand and wondering about their future. They had enough money to go "home", and while that was tempting, they liked their present location. They had surely had their plans derailed, but they were looking ahead to what they could do.

Stan and Marcy were looking through the last box of funny papers, and magazines that Ken had sent down. There was a personal letter from the insurance company that insured their stuff at the storage place in the states. Piecing everything together, they saw that the professional storage place, which they had been paying for all this time, had been broken into. The thieves broke into a gun cabinet and evidently emptied it out. To conceal the evidence, they then burnt the place down. Stan's racing bike, the dinghy he had in high school, and all his trophies were gone, along with Marcy's wedding dress. His Coast Guard sword, and uniforms, which no longer fit, were also gone. By now their attitude was; we have lived without that stuff all this time, why do we need them now? Ken had contacted the storage place, and the extra insurance for the bike and dinghy had increased their settlement check. All that was left was their marriage album. Later when they saw it, it was charred around the edges. They sat there with the thought, "Welcome to the Caribbean!!"

Then they noticed the boat coming into the harbor towing a boat that looked familiar. It was *Susan*!! They could hardly believe it. The mast was gone, the top was ripped off, but there she was floating on the end of a tow line. The boat doing the towing was not as big as *Susan*, but was a typical Japanese fishing boat. Long and narrow, it took a small engine to push through the water. It docked at the Coast Guard Station, near Frazer's marina.

They didn't need a real close look to recognize the boat that they had literally put together.

"Looks like *Susan* has returned to our lives." Marcy said.

"Maybe, but it's going to take more work."

"So, work, and time, we have, and we have some money." Marcy queried.

"Maybe, it won't cost too much to fix."

"I can think of worse places in the world to be stranded. But, we are not stranded; we can make some choices here."

"If we can get *Susan* back cheap enough, we could maybe make Al an offer and this time work on our own boat." Stan suggested.

Marcy liked that idea. "Maybe Frazer could talk to the boat's captain, and just maybe we could get a great deal."

They quickly folded up their towels and went to get Frazer. They had learned the best way to work with local people was to use other local people, especially when money was involved.

Generally the seller saw a foreigner and the price jumped considerably.

Frazer went over to talk to the captain of the boat that had found *Susan* floating in the ocean. Was he going to claim salvage? Frazer had been glad for the Kerry's to be around and was willing to do them a favor. He found the fisherman who towed *Susan* in.

Frazer began the conversation with talk about the weather, and the fishing. Finally he said, "Where did you find the boat you towed in."

"Saw her drifting out west. Had no mast, and no cabin top. No one around, so I put a line on it and brought it home." The fisherman Marcus replied.

"What are you going to do with it?"

Marcus said he really didn't know. "The Coast Guard were highly interested in it and had impounded it. They said they had to find the owners of the boat. One of the Coast Guard people had seen the boat over at Frazer's and had talked several times with the couple that worked on it, but boat and the couple had been gone for several weeks."

"So will you get it eventually?" Frazer asked.

Marcus replied, "They said I can't claim salvage until at least a year goes by. But the boat has a registration number on the front bulkhead, and they would have to make some inquiries."

Frazer remarked that indeed the couple had worked on the boat. Frazer had seen the inside of *Susan*. With it now exposed to the rain, and water already in the bilge he ventured a guess that in a year's time it wouldn't be worth very much.

Marcus then observed, "Even if I got it, I would have to haul it out of the water on lift or rail, like you have, and that would cost money. Then I would have to work on it cause I couldn't afford to hire anyone. And with the cabin top and the mast gone, it is going to cost big bucks to fix."

"What happens if the owners were found?" Frazer asked.

"Then I could only charge them what it cost to tow." Marcus replied.

"How much would that be? How far out did you take it in tow?"

Marcus then admitted he probably only used about 20 gallons of gas. Frazer said he would be willing to pay for that and an extra $100 for the salvage rights to the boat.

Marcus always living from fishing day to fishing day, agreed to the terms.

Frazer walked over to the Coast Guard Station and told them the people who were on the boat, were here in St. Vincent, and would like their boat back. For a small fee the Coast Guard agreed that would be a good idea. They wanted to hear the entire story of how the boat got damaged, and became adrift. Frazer set up a time for them to come over and be interviewed.

They knew that if anything could be worked out, they were going to fix up *Susan* again, and finish the trip they had started. They called Al and let him know the latest developments. They found out that Al had activated the insurance policy, just before they launched, which he had not told them he had done. He would be the beneficiary of it. When they first called him a week ago, he had contacted the insurance company and they had already paid him for the missing boat.

At this point, Stan and Marcy asked Al to sell them the boat outright. When he balked at that idea they reminded him of the labor they had already poured into the boat, and it was in need of more work and materials before the boat could go anywhere. They were not ready to work more on *Susan* unless they owned it. They would just catch a flight back to the U.S. On the phone Al decided that getting the insurance money, plus a little more from them, was the best deal he could get. A few faxes back and forth and *Susan* had new owners.

They also found out that Al had bought a third boat. It was a classic wooden boat that had raced successfully in the Bermuda race and won its class several times. What the seller didn't know, before the deal was complete, Al had a company that wanted to lease the boat for Caribbean charter for its VIPs. They paid enough cash up front for Al to buy the boat. They would get it for several years, and at the end of the time, return the boat in A-1 condition. They didn't know that Al wasn't the owner until after they paid him. By then he had used their money to buy the boat. So now he was the owner, and they had already signed a contract for use of the boat. Selling *Susan* was just a good business deal at this point, and one less boat to worry about.

Frazer pulled the boat out of the water and set it in the same spot it had rested before. Work began as soon as it was securely in its old position. Everything was stripped out of the boat and stored away after fresh water wash down and drying out. The cans had lost all their labels. They had used a magic marker and by labeling all the cans, they still knew what was inside. They began using the canned goods almost immediately. Fresh water would not really stop the process of rust that had already begun to show on some cans. Eventually all the remaining cans would rust.

The internal bulkheads, lockers, shelves and bunks would not need rebuilding. The deck was still good; it was just the cabin top that was showing any structured damage. The equipment for such a boat could cost them plenty. As they had equipped the boat, they had a very good idea of what was aboard. They even got back the electronics, and navigational equipment: parallel rulers, dividers, compass and charts.

Stan and Marcy decided that anybody can come to the Caribbean and go sailing; but they had had an adventure. And they realized that it was not going to stop, it was going to keep going. Rebuilding the boat began to progress. Now that they had done it once, doing it the second time was faster and easier. Hurricanes steered clear of them as they prepared *Susan* for the sea.

Epilogue

Two weeks after I got my driver's license, I got my first speeding ticket. It was late at night, and my mom had reminded me that I needed to take a friend of ours home. Enroute to his house, we were talking and I failed to see the speed limit sign. The area was not in a housing area, but surrounded on both sides by tall grassy farmland. I got the ticket for doing 35 in a 25 zone.

My father went with me to court. The judge was very fair, but I had broken the law. Even though my speeding was not intentional, I was speeding. Guilty as charged. The fine was $10 and I reached for my wallet. My father standing there, said, "Let me pay for it." I was so glad for him to do that. I knew I didn't have a dime on me.

At the end of the day, I was guilty as charged even though I didn't do it on purpose. A penalty had to be paid. A fair, honest and righteous judge couldn't just say, "I forgive you." He had to follow the letter of the law. I was unable to pay. There was no way I could have paid the fine on my own. My father paid for me. Because I agreed to let him do that, I was free to leave, because my father paid for me.

The Bible declares all are sinners in the eyes of a Holy God. Whether we intend to or not, we have sinned. Falling short of the standards given by a holy God, we have failed.

I went to church faithfully, was even President of my Sunday School Class. I had already been baptized, but one day realized I couldn't answer the question, "If you died today where would you spend eternity?"

I was already a member of the church and remember talking to a deacon about eternity. I talked to my father. But I had no definitive answer.

It was one night after a guest speaker had spoken that my pastor got up and said, 'Are you 100% sure you would go to heaven if you died tonight?"

The Holy Spirit said in my heart, "You aren't sure, are you?"

"No, I am not sure." Was my reply.

"If you are not sure, why don't you settle it tonight?" The Pastor said.

"Why don't you?" The Holy Spirit asked.

As the church sang I went forward. The pastor acted surprised to see me, and asked what I came for. I told him I was not sure I would go to heaven. I don't remember all the Bible verses he showed me.

1) I know that night I realized I was a sinner. Romans 3:10 "As it is written, There is none righteous, no, not one:" and again Romans 3:23 "For all have sinned, and come short of the glory of God;"

2) That I was guilty before a holy God. James 2:10 "For whosoever shall keep the whole law, and yet offend in one point, he is guilty of all."

3) That I needed to respond now: Isaiah 55:6 "Seek ye the LORD while he may be found, call ye upon him while he is near:"

4) Jesus would pay my debt, if I would just ask Him. 1John 2:2 "And he is the propitiation for our sins: and not for ours only, but also for the sins of the whole world."

5) That night I got on my knees and asked Jesus to save me, and He did!! Romans 10: 9-10 "That if thou shalt confess with thy mouth the Lord Jesus, and shalt believe in thine heart that God hath raised him from the dead, thou shalt be saved. For with the heart man believeth unto righteousness; and with the mouth confession is made unto salvation." And again in Romans 10:13 "For whosoever shall call upon the name of the Lord shall be saved."

As simply as asking my father to pay my fine in a court of law on this earth, I asked Jesus to pay my debt in heaven's court of law. And He did.

That step of faith to give my heart and life to Jesus changed my life forever (Literally and figuratively).

Eternity is a long time, compared to life's short while. In this book I have given experience after experience where life could have been over. Through no effort of mine, I am still alive. But if as they say in St. Vincent "When time turns into eternity" where will you be? When I was 12 years old, I was already a member of a church, baptized, and faithfully attended church. But I was not saved.

God loves you (John 3:16). You are guilty in your sins before God. A just, fair, righteous God cannot excuse sin, and say, "I forgive you." The sin debt has to be paid. Jesus paid it for you. I urge you to make the transaction, and confess your sin before God, and ask for Jesus' blood to atone for your sins, before "Time turns into eternity."

If you would like to contact the author we should be reachable at: microvincy@yahoo.com

Or go through our website: http://alanberry.wix.com/alan-and-beverly-berry#!

Find our website by Googling, or Ask, or Bing, or Yahoo: Alan and Beverly Berry. We generally are in the top three answers.

My Definitions!

Starboard – right side of the boat

Port – the other side of the boat

Bow – front of the boat, the pointy end

Cockpit – where everybody sits when on deck

Companion way - generally a short ladder connecting the "down below" area with the cockpit.

Draft – how deep the water has to be to float the boat

E.C. – Eastern Caribbean currency

    $1.00 U.S. =$ 2.67 E.C.
    $38.00U.S.= about $100 E.C.
    $20 U.S. = about $50.00 E.C.

Fathometer - An instrument that tells you how deep the water is underneath the boat

Fetch – distance between the tops of the waves

Forestay – the wire in the front of the boat, keeping the mast from falling backwards

Backstay – the wire that runs towards the back that prevents the mast from falling forward

Sidestay – Wires on each side of the mast to prevent it from falling sideways off the boat.

Midship – in the middle of the ship/boat/yacht

Painter – rope at the front of a dinghy

RIB – Rigid Inflatable Boat

Sea anchor – something like a parachute that is deployed in the water in bad weather, and acts like an anchor, even though it doesn't reach the ground.

Wake – disturbance left in the water after a boat passes through

Windscreen – windshield

In this digital world I have to include this definition: clockwise direction – it is the direction the hands went on an old fashioned clock. They would turn going from left to right.